VAMP

Books by Loren D. Estleman

AMOS WALKER MYSTERIES

Motor City Blue
Angel Eyes
The Midnight Man
The Glass Highway
Sugartown
Every Brilliant Eye
Lady Yesterday
Downriver
Silent Thunder
Sweet Women Lie

Never Street
The Witchfinder
The Hours of the Virgin
A Smile on the Face
of the Tiger
Sinister Heights
Poison Blonde*
Retro*
Nicotine Kiss*
American Detective*

The Left-Handed Dollar*
Infernal Angels*
Burning Midnight*
Don't Look for Me*
You Know Who Killed Me*
The Sundown Speech*
The Lioness Is the Hunter*
Black and White Ball*
When Old Midnight
Comes Along*
Cutthroat Dogs*
Monkey in the Middle*

VALENTINO, FILM DETECTIVE

Frames*
Alone*

Alive!*
Shoot*
Vamp*

Brazen*
Indigo*

DETROIT CRIME

Whiskey River
Motown

King of the Corner
Edsel
Thunder City*

Stress
Jitterbug*

PETER MACKLIN

Kill Zone
Roses Are Dead

Any Man's Death
Something Borrowed,
Something Black*

Little Black Dress*

OTHER FICTION

The Oklahoma Punk
Sherlock Holmes vs.
Dracula
Dr. Jekyll and Mr. Holmes
Peeper

Gas City*
Journey of the Dead*
The Rocky Mountain
Moving Picture Association*
Roy & Lillie: A Love Story*

The Confessions of Al
Capone*

PAGE MURDOCK SERIES

The High Rocks*
Stamping Ground*
Murdock's Law*

The Stranglers
City of Widows*
White Desert*
Wild Justice*

Port Hazard*
The Book of Murdock*
Cape Hell*

WESTERNS

The Hider
Aces & Eights*
The Wolfer
Mister St. John
This Old Bill
Gun Man
Bloody Season

Sudden Country
Billy Gashade*
The Master Executioner*
Black Powder, White
Smoke*
The Undertaker's Wife*

The Adventures of Johnny
Vermillion*
The Branch and the
Scaffold*
Ragtime Cowboys*
The Long High Noon*
The Ballad of Black Bart*

NONFICTION

The Wister Trace

Writing the Popular Novel

*Published by Tor Publishing Group

LOREN D. ESTLEMAN

VAMP

A VALENTINO MYSTERY

TOR PUBLISHING GROUP

NEW YORK

VAMP

A Forge Book
Published by Tor Publishing Group / Tom Doherty Associates
120 Broadway
New York, NY 10271

www.tor-forge.com

Forge® is a registered trademark of Macmillan Publishing Group, LLC.

The Library of Congress Cataloging-in-Publication Data is
available upon request.

ISBN 978-1-250-89247-8 (hardcover)
ISBN 978-1-250-89248-5 (ebook)

Our books may be purchased in bulk for promotional, educational, or business
use. Please contact your local bookseller or the Macmillan Corporate and
Premium Sales Department at 1-800-221-7945, extension 5442, or by email at
MacmillanSpecialMarkets@macmillan.com.

First Edition: 2023

Printed in the United States of America

0 9 8 7 6 5 4 3 2 1

To Jim O'Keefe:
A loyal friend and a gifted artist

Vamp, *n.* Short for VAMPIRE. *n.*, 2; in jocose use, one who uses her charm or wiles to gain admiration and attentions from the opposite sex. *Slang.*

—Webster's New International Dictionary of the English Language, Second Edition UNABRIDGED

Once you reach the sky, you don't want to come down again.

—Theda Bara, 1919

VAMP

I

RUSSIAN TO
JUDGMENT

1

ONE FOOT OVER the threshold of her condominium, Harriet Johansen leaned back to confirm the number on the door.

"I thought I got off the elevator on four by mistake," she said. "My neighbor there scrubs biochemical labs for a living."

Valentino grinned. "I just tidied up a little."

She looked around. The hours she spent working with the LAPD forensics team hadn't trained her in housekeeping. She was a minimalist by necessity, furnishing her home in Spartan fashion: There wasn't a knickknack or a throw rug or a decorative pillow in the place. You could sweep it out with a leafblower. Nevertheless, stale air, gray film, and garments shed in a hurry had managed to breed and multiply like rabbits—or more accurately, dust bunnies. Unavoidable neglect was the cause, and the arrival of a roommate with more time on his hands the cure. The flat smelled of Febreze and Lemon Pledge and shone as bright as new chrome.

She looked down at her feet. "I own a carpet shampooer?"

"I rented it. I churned up enough popcorn kernels to stock the concession stand in the Oracle for a year."

"If I knew I was going to live with Howard Hughes, I'd have told you to check into a Motel Six."

He took off his apron and used it to wipe his hands. "You're not pleased."

"I don't mind so much that you're Felix Unger as the suggestion that I'm Oscar Madison. I put in more hours at work on a regular basis than you did even when you were up to your neck in asbestos and horsehair plaster in your theater. When there's a gang uprising in East L.A., I only stop by to change clothes before I go back to opening up cadavers."

"I know that. Since you won't let me help out with the mortgage, making myself useful is the next best thing. I didn't reorganize the kitchen," he added quickly. "I know how important it is to you to know your way around."

"I couldn't care less if the potato masher's where the sieve should be. Little Caesar feeds me most of the time." She shrugged out of her jacket, made a move to toss it on the sofa, then stopped and folded it over her arm. "Just tell me you didn't change anything in the bathroom."

"I was afraid to touch the jars and bottles. I don't know what half that stuff is for."

"No, and you never will, if we ever decide to cohabit permanently. I prefer to be a woman of mystery."

Their living arrangement was temporary. The Oracle, the old motion-picture palace Valentino had been restoring through the last three presidential administrations, was undergoing yet more construction to build a proper bathroom onto the projection booth he used as a living quarters. Previously, he'd freshened up in one of the customers' rest rooms; but technological advances had allowed him to replace the ancient gravity-operated water heater in the utility room next door to the booth with a state-of-the-art unit in the basement and install facilities on the floor where he slept.

It had turned out to be a not-so-mini-reunion with the civic and construction migraines that had accompanied the original project. That situation had been exacerbated by a megalomaniac theater designer, a crooked building inspector, and a series of murders to solve—on amateur detective Valentino's part, not professional Harriet's.

He stepped forward, holding out a hand. She gave him the jacket with her police ID clipped to it. He opened the closet, hung it up, and shut the door before she could see how he'd rearranged everything by color and season. "Does a steady diet of pizza mean you'd rather pass on lasagna?"

She sniffed the air. "That doesn't smell like Stouffer's."

"Sue me. My grandmother was half Italian."

"My *great*-grandmother was Cherokee; you know, the tribe where when the woman got fed up, she piled all her husband's belongings outside the lodge and that was the end of the relationship. Let that be a lesson to you." She smiled and went up on tiptoe to kiss him. "I'm starving."

"Good. I made enough for a regiment. I should explain my grandmother ran a restaurant. She couldn't cook for any group fewer than a hundred." He pulled her chair out from the cloth-covered dining table and held it for her.

They'd finished the salad and he was dishing up the entrée when a tinny orchestra started playing "Saturday Night at the Movies." Valentino said, "That's mine."

"No kidding." Harriet's ring tone was the elevator song that had come with her phone.

He got out his and looked at the screen. "Dinky Schwartz. I haven't heard from him since my sophomore year."

"I'm sure there's a cute story behind how he got the nickname."

"It's on his birth certificate." He excused himself and answered.

Still famished, she tuned out the "How-are-you-and-what-have-you-been-up-to" portion of the conversation and dove into her lasagna, washing it down with a California rosé. She glanced up during the hemming-and-hawing on Valentino's end. Finally he said, "Dinky, I don't know. I can't promise anything. I'll get back to you."

He punched out, frowning at the object in his hand as if it were a jury summons. "You're in danger of reestablishing your relationship with Little Caesar," he said, looking up.

"A funeral?"

"Worse. Dinky's bought a movie theater and he wants me to help restore it."

2

DINKY SCHWARTZ'S PARENTS had a twisted sense of humor; otherwise they wouldn't have given him that name based on his premature birth weight of less than two pounds. Fate—and an impressive growth spurt in high school—had turned what may have seemed a cruel joke into a party-pleaser whenever he entered the room.

At nineteen, he'd stood six-three and weighed two hundred ten pounds, most of it in his chest and shoulders. His size and strength had earned him a place in the line on the Bruins' second string, but his lack of coordination (and a humiliating finish in the fifty-yard dash) had denied him a scholarship. He'd dropped out of UCLA in his second year to work in construction.

A sign posted in front of a recently demolished building downtown read:

FUTURE SITE OF JUBILACIÓN ARMS, A PLACE FOR SE-
NIORS TO RESIDE IN 70 STORIES OF DIGNITY AND LUXURY
D. SCHWARTZ CONTRACTORS, INC.

Stepping through the opening in the board fence surrounding the property, Valentino reflected that his old friend's dreams of gridiron glory had turned into what must be a comforting reality. The property, located equidistant from Beverly Hills and South Pasadena, was worth many millions (especially considering the likely wherewithal of its prospective tenants), and whoever owned it wouldn't award the building contract to just anyone.

To all appearances, Dinky had recruited his crew from his old defensive line. A man of average height could not wander among those giants in hard hats without wondering if he'd shrunk since breakfast. One, whose thick bony ridge of forehead made his protective headgear seem redundant, pointed his steaming Starbuck's cup toward a plywood trailer on the northeast corner of the lot. A monster diesel pickup with tractor-size tires was parked next to it, gleaming show-floor new.

"Val! You haven't changed a bit!"

But Dinky had, some. The man who leapt up from behind a steel desk to shake his hand had put on an extra twenty or so pounds, mostly around his waist, and grown a second chin; however, the eyes embedded in his broad red face twinkled with youth, and his grip could still crush a bowling ball. His visitor was still trying to shake circulation back into his hand when the contractor swept a stack of blueprints off a folding chair for him to sit.

"You look good, Dink. I've seen your signs all around town. I never put D. SCHWARTZ together with my old study partner."

"Partner, hell!" Schwartz straddled his seat. "If you hadn't stepped in as my unofficial tutor, I'd have flunked out before my first practice. It bought me time to consider my options. If not for you I'd be one of those fat losers you see guzzling beer in sports bars, gassing about the touchdown they scored in the big game against Podunk State."

"Nobody'd ever mistake you for one of those."

"You either. Seems I can't go online without seeing your kisser next to the title of some movie I never heard of. You must be head of the department by now. Remember old man Broadhead? I bet they buried him with a stake through the heart."

"Actually, he's still head of the department. We work together."

Schwartz's mouth dropped open, exposing expensive dental work; Valentino missed the familiar old gap in his front teeth, a mark of character. "No kidding! What is he, a hundred?"

"That's what I drew in the pool."

"I was looking for the easy A when I took his course. Who'd think film history was so much like math? All those dates and running times and three minutes' difference in footage between the rough cut and the release. See, I still remember the language. It's like having a song you can't ditch, running over and over in your head."

The film archivist decided the time for reminiscing was past. "I remember you never had much interest in the subject. That's one of the reasons I was so surprised when you called, and what about."

"It's a pain in the butt is what it is. A shopping mall I built went belly up even before it opened and the syndicate that hired me to build it couldn't come through on the last payment, a biggie. Back when they were flush, they bought a drive-in theater that busted flat under Nixon, thinking to sell it to Walmart for a superstore, only Walmart backed out, which I'm guessing is part of the reason the syndicate's in Chapter Eleven. Anyway we cut a deal: I get twenty acres in the Valley, and I don't wait in line behind a thousand creditors waiting to get my fifteen cents on the dollar."

"But why build another drive-in, if the first one failed?"

"Well, the original plan was to doze what's left of it—heck, it's just a ticket booth and a concession hut and a few hundred speaker posts, Lord knows what became of the screen—and throw up a housing development; but rezoning's a nightmare. And then there's this." He opened the top drawer of the desk, took something out, and slapped it down on his guest's lap.

Valentino recognized the white-on-red masthead before he read it. It was an issue of *Parade* magazine from the third week of July, showing a couple snuggling in a convertible facing an enormous outdoor screen showing a scene from *Star Wars*. DRIVE-INS THEN & NOW read the legend superimposed on the image, and below in smaller type *The Comeback of an American Treasure*.

"I snitched it from my dentist's waiting room," Schwartz said. "My tablet went dead or I'd never have picked it up. Talk about kismet!"

Little about the evolution of film escaped Valentino: He'd seen the issue when it came with the Sunday *Times*, but he opened it to the cover article and read it once again. It trumpeted the renaissance of the open-air movie theater, an icon of the Atomic Age. At the height of the Baby Boom, families migrated to rural America to watch movies on a huge outdoor screen, devouring splashy Biblical epics, juvenile delinquent exposés, rock operas, and a menagerie of Martian invaders, gigantic insects, and fifty-foot women, all without leaving the car. On Saturday night, the roads resembled a key scene from *Exodus*.

The American Drive-In Theater had surfaced during the Great Depression, treaded water throughout World War II, then crested with the rise of post-war suburbia. But then a slew of social changes—soaring gas prices and smaller, more cramped automobiles, to name just two—pulled the plug. Multi-screen cineplexes, shopping malls, fast-food restaurants, and covered sports arenas took over the sites.

Valentino looked up. "Says here they're due for a comeback.

Social distancing and drive-in entertainment were made for each other."

"*Plus* you can stretch out your legs in an SUV and listen to surround sound on kick-ass factory speakers. Val, I'm telling you—"

"Hang on, Dink. This is just a feel-good summer feature the editors dug up from the file, not a crystal ball. Five years ago, the industry predicted that all motion pictures would be shot in three-D by the end of the decade. Didn't happen. I'm big on all things movie, but I can't advise an old friend to risk everything based on a puff piece in a Sunday magazine." He leaned forward and laid *Parade* on the desk.

But Schwartz's eyes were still bright. He spread the magazine back open and flicked sausage fingers at a sidebar item. "Here's one in Pennsylvania; been going since nineteen-thirty-four. Maryland; triple features seven days a week. Oregon; sixty-seven years and counting. Idaho; started under Truman, still going strong. Another one in Pennsylvania—"

"All pre-existing concerns. They paid off their debts decades ago; the rest is just upkeep. As long as they maintain a steady trickle of business, they can keep their heads above water. They're surviving, not prospering. Starting a museum piece from scratch is a dangerous gamble. I'm an expert on that, believe me. It's like investing in a Model-T factory just because people cheer whenever a tin lizzie shows up in a parade."

"Those debts were mortgages on the original land purchases. I own this place free and clear. I'm way ahead of where you were when you decided to turn a rat-trap into a palace. No offense! Look what you've done with it."

"The jury's still out on whether it was all worth it. I'm still not in the black."

"I knew I could count on honesty from you. But consider this: What if, a few years ago, you sank a couple thousand bucks in one of the last recording studios that stamped out thirty-three-and-a-third RPM records? Folks would say you were nuts! Have you been to Best Buy lately, asked them where they keep the CDs?

"*I* did," he said, before Valentino could respond. "The clerk said they didn't carry 'em anymore, told me to check out their LP section. And reissues are only part of the package. Even rappers are putting their stuff on vinyl. By now, that two grand would put you in a tax bracket with Bill Gates!"

"But we're not talking two grand, are we? You can't just throw up a bedsheet screen, stick box speakers up on poles, sell popcorn and candy and sodas from a plywood hut, and expect miracles. Today's audiences need more than that to get them off their Lay-Z-Boys and out of the house."

"See, that's where I need your advice. It's all still fresh in your mind."

"Outdoor entertaining is a different dynamic. Retrofitting a vintage drive-in to accommodate twenty-first-century tastes will cost you a lot more than just two grand."

The contractor sat back, folding his huge hands across his paunch. His smile was almost too broad for his jack-o'-lantern-size face.

"I got a lot more than two grand, Val. You work with me on this, I'll put enough in your pocket to build ten more Oracles from scratch."

3

VALENTINO'S PULSE ACCELERATED. He had no intention of subjecting himself to ten challenges like The Oracle; the distractions had nearly cost him his job at the university and his relationship with Harriet. But there might be enough profit in it to upgrade his sound equipment and possibly buy a commercial-grade laser projector. A demonstration he'd seen had made *The Big Parade* look as if the First World War were being fought in his lap.

But he shook his head.

"There's a world of difference between designing a drive-in and an indoor theater. I'm not sure even the expert who helped me through mine would know where to start. I don't think I could live with myself if I drove you into bankruptcy."

"I'm a grown man, Val. I lived on baloney sandwiches while I was getting this business off the ground. But don't underestimate yourself. You got me through American History, and I didn't know General Washington from General Mills. Talk to your guy, see what he thinks. I'll stand the fee for the consultation, even if the answer's no."

He was steeled to refuse; but it felt like walking away from a puppy wagging its tail in a pound.

"I'll talk to him. If the answer's no, he won't charge a dime. I have to warn you, though: If it's yes, his fee will be the smallest part of the expense. You may have to build a dozen skyscrapers to stay afloat."

"If this works out, I've climbed my last high-rise. At least I won't get a nosebleed looking at an overdue bill." Schwartz leaned close and squeezed Valentino's knee, cutting off the blood flow like a steel clamp. "Let me know what he says, yes, no, or go to hell."

"*Da* or *nyet*, actually. I don't know the Russian for go to hell."

The hand was withdrawn, making his leg tingle. "Commie?"

"Don't think Stalin. Think Ivan the Terrible."

"Get him too. Money's no object."

RUTH, WHO RAN the reception area at UCLA's Film and TV Preservation Department with an iron hand in a steel glove, didn't look up from her computer when Valentino asked if Kyle Broadhead was available. A lacquered nail as long and sharp as a surgeon's lancet pointed toward the door to the professor's office. "Unless he's dead."

"I heard that," came a voice from the other side of the door.

"Did I whisper?"

Broadhead was, of course, available. His personal blend of pipe tobacco befouled the air in the converted power plant from cock's-crow to owl's-hoot, unless he was off on some rare and mysterious excursion; but to take him for granted was as severe an infraction as asking him where he went when he went.

Valentino entered without knocking. Of all those who worked on campus, he was the only one awarded the privilege. He asked when his mentor would get around to putting his name on the door. It had been blank ever since he'd moved in.

Broadhead, balancing his chair backward on two wheels, blew a plume at the perfect circle of stain on the ceiling. "Once again, the Board of Regents is considering my dismissal."

"What for this time?"

"Take your pick. Insubordination, probably, if not outright insurrection. An ornament of this institution dangles from a single human hair, inches from shattering in a thousand pieces."

"Hogwash. You attained tenure before I was born."

"Tenure be damned. I'm a pariah, and I worked harder for that." He leaned forward and dumped his ashes out onto the desktop. There they smoldered until Valentino snatched a pencil out of its cup and tamped out the sparks with the eraser.

"Are you trying to burn the place down?"

"As well as set fire to Ruth. They're both insulated with asbestos."

"I heard that," she said from outside.

"Did I whisper?"

The professor of cinema history was built along the lines of an oil drum, his eyebrows threatening to entangle themselves with his grizzle of hair. His tweed jacket and sweater vest held as much ash as the tray on his desk. The tray, a battered circle of brass, was the butt end of a mortar shell, a souvenir of his tenancy in a political prison in Tito's Yugoslavia; or had come from an Army and Navy store in San Diego. If half the stories he told of his youth were true, the suspiciously smudged birth year in his personnel file would have to start with 18.

"I need advice." Valentino took a seat in the only other chair, Mission Oak and uncompromising. Broadhead's office was spare, unlike his own, which was a dumpsite of aging fan magazines, thumb-worn movie scripts, and Hollywood memorabilia from the days of the silents to the age of CGI. The only things the department head never threw away were his wardrobe and that gnarled twist of charred briar cooling in the tray.

"Write to Dear Abby, if she still exists. I never give advice."

"Except when someone asks, or you decide to do it anyway."

"Fire away, grasshopper, and don't tarry. I've a class to teach in an hour."

"I thought you only showed up on the first and last day of the term."

"My T.A. ruptured his appendix. His medical team expects him to recover, but they won't let me into the ICU to go over the syllabus with him. He smuggled in two Charles Higham titles against my specific instructions."

Valentino didn't rise to that bait. If it pleased his oldest acquaintance to deceive the world into labeling him a heartless academic, it wasn't the archivist's responsibility to challenge him. In as few words as possible he recounted his meeting with the contractor and waited for his opinion.

"What was his name again?"

"Dinky Schwartz. You wouldn't remember him. He—"

"Does he still think Bull Montana led the Forty-Niners to four Super Bowl championships?"

Valentino was less impressed that Broadhead knew Joe Montana's career record than that he remembered a student he'd taught more than a dozen years ago. "How could you pick him out from the hundreds who've sat in your class since?"

"You don't meet many Dinkys in the circles I move in; but that's only part of it. I livened up my share of cocktail fundraisers telling stories about the undergrad who didn't know RKO from the NFL. Your friend may claim credit for the climate-control system in the film lab. Some of our wealthy donors actually know a bit about the lively arts."

"So what do you think?"

"I think that when he learned to read a blueprint, this university lost a worthy candidate for president."

"You know what I mean."

"I've a special place in my heart for drive-ins. I proposed to my first wife in a 'sixty-three Corvair at the Dixie Car-ena in Santa Monica between reels of *Barbarella*. I should include a chapter in my book speculating how many unions were conceived during bad movies."

He'd been writing a companion piece to his groundbreaking *Persistence of Vision* for nearly as many years as Valentino had been tinkering with The Oracle; or claiming to be writing it. No one had yet to see so much as a paragraph, as far as his protégé knew.

"Does that mean you approve?"

"Decidedly, emphatically, manifestly not. The Car-ena, which had been in business since Eisenhower was a shavetail, didn't last any longer than that particular matrimonial blunder. The gas crisis of 'seventy-three finished it off—the drive-in, not the marriage; that was stillborn. By then the enterprise had been shambling along muttering to itself like the walking dead for years. It was a mercy killing."

"Dinky says the concept's ripe for a comeback. He's not a castle-in-the-sky kind of guy. This town's filled with landmarks he built."

"L.A. has no landmarks, only placeholders for the next Tim Horton's. I give him credit for stumbling onto the best continuous source of income since the vending machine, but he knows less about the entertainment business than I do about cordless drills. He can afford to take a bath. You've got all you can do to keep from going down that drain of yours in West Hollywood."

"I really thought you'd made your peace with that." Broadhead—and Fanta, his youthful bride—had been instrumental in organizing a party commemorating Valentino's grand opening only a few months earlier.

"I have," said his friend; and assumed the once-in-a-blue-moon expression of compassion that generally put his enemies on guard. "It's just that I've seen too many bright hopes in this business turn to offal in a blink. Last week I took lunch at the Brass Gimbal, and eavesdropped on a table of continuity writers and assistant second-unit directors still talking about the same big-money deal they were talking about a year ago. It was enough to put me off my James Wong Howe Dim Sum. I've rooted for you in secret all these years; you might thank me for shoring you up with my doomsday prognostications, when honest sympathy would've made you drop the whole business."

"Is that what you're doing now?"

"I can be sincere, no matter what you hear around that board table." Which was hardly an answer. "Through a combination of luck, mulishness, and applied naïveté, you succeeded, where the moneybags who built that white elephant failed on the grand scale. A year from now, with A-listers queued up around the block to watch the premiere of the eleventh chapter of *Fast and Furious* at the Oracle and your face on the cover of *Forbes*, I'll serve a slice of humble pie to each of the bankers who denied you a loan; and if you throw in with Bob the Builder over this latest disaster and wind up living in your car, I'll help you out. But I won't encourage you, even with hilarious assumptions about the insanity that runs in the Valentino family.

"No battle plan survives the first engagement with the enemy," he went on; "the enemy in this case being hard fact. Everybody's in favor of reviving fine old institutions like the drive-in theater. Nobody's going to spend a dime on a ticket after the novelty wears off. A car is no longer just transportation, Val. It's a rolling entertainment center; multiplex, sports arena, and rock concert house all in one—better, because it can take you somewhere else the minute you get bored. You can recline on your heated seat or in Arctic air-conditioning listening to Caruso, Crosby, and Kill-Z piped in over six speakers by way of Sirius, sipping a Mocha Grande brewed up in the dashboard while you review your portfolio on the Tokyo Stock Exchange. America's love affair with the automobile is history. We take it for granted, like a spouse with all the mystery wrung out. It parks itself, it drives itself, it tells us where to go, how to get there, and when we've arrived. We're not about to shut off all our magic gizmos to watch Seth Rogen pick his nose on a screen as big as San Diego in a half-empty parking lot. We can get that on a cozy flip-down monitor in the front seat."

After Broadhead finished—more from having run out of wind than arguments in favor of his theory—Valentino sat silent, deflated. Finally he shook himself and rose. "The regents aren't seriously thinking of letting you go, are they?"

"They're nothing if not serious. Have you ever seen such a group of pickle-pusses outside a sardine hatchery? They'll try to make me think it's my idea by offering me a severance package with zeroes enough to endow a new school of medicine, but I'll turn it down. I don't need money. I'm married to a lawyer."

He looked suddenly contrite; or contrived to. He was as indecipherable as a P.A. announcement at LAX. "I'm sorry, Val. You wanted to put on a show in your dad's barn and I burned it to the ground."

"To be honest, I was hoping you'd do just that. A man's entitled to only one catastrophe in his life. Only a fool would expect the sun to shine on him twice."

"No thanks necessary. I'm here all week." The professor picked up his pipe, felt the bowl, and began filling it from the drawer he used as a humidor, chock full of loose tobacco. "I expect free passes for Fanta and me when you open the place."

4

HE PAUSED AT Ruth's doughnut-shaped command station, where she was holding up a sheaf of messages, torn from a pad originally headed WHILE YOU WERE OUT DICKING AROUND; a gift from Kyle Broadhead. The last two words were whited out. She despised levity but refused to throw away perfectly good stationery.

In his office, Valentino distributed the sheets between the mound of paper on his desk and the wastebasket. The thorny receptionist weeded out calls for political action, sales pitches, and warnings that a credit-card account he didn't have had been hacked; but even someone as marginally connected with the entertainment business as a film archivist had to deal with his share of self-promoting dross. A faded porn star wanted to offer his grainy *oeuvre* to the university for restoration and preservation; a film exhibitor in Fresno said he had a line on *Number Thirteen*, Alfred Hitchcock's first film; an attorney in Miami had a bone to pick with him about the rights to *Greed*; and someone who wouldn't leave his name, only a telephone number, wanted to meet with him privately in regard to *Cleopatra*.

The dirty-picture offer went into the wastebasket immediately, followed by the Kleenex he used to wipe his hands afterward. The Florida lawyer was probably a shyster sniffing around for a settlement to make him go away, but Valentino kept that message to pass along to Smith Oldfield in Legal. He held onto the *Number Thirteen* tease also, even though he averaged three leads a year to that long-lost uncut gem, none of which ever panned out. *Cleopatra* disappeared, quicker than a strike from an asp, without a glance at the phone number. That four-hour turkey had nearly sunk 20th Century Fox in 1963; he wasn't about to expose his department to the Curse of the Pharaohs.

His gaze fell to the bill spindle perched on a pile of yellowed press kits. Dinky Schwartz's business card was skewered topmost. Looking up, Valentino caught his reflection in the glazed frame of a studio photo signed by Mae West. His face looked lost. Mae's looked scornful.

Still burning under her judgment, he got out his phone and scrolled down to a number he'd planned to eliminate from his speed dial now that The Oracle was up and running.

"If I am not the party you seek, please to hang up," said the guttural voice that answered. "If I am, please to leave a message. Do not abuse this gift of my time."

The recording was no surprise. Leo Kalishnikov, the most famous theater designer in California (he would say the world) was never available. He was always prancing through some bat-infested shell in Burbank or sketching frescoes in Rome.

"Leo, this is Val—"

"Valentino! *Tovarich!* This is divine intervention. I was just now poised to summon you!"

Startled, he looked again at Mae West. Her expression now was smug.

KALISHNIKOV WOULD ONLY discuss what was on his mind in person, and hung up before Valentino could counter with a request of his own. That was typical of a white Russian who claimed he'd defected to the U.S. shortly before the Soviet Union collapsed. His on-again, off-again client was curious enough to hear him out. The old rooster might return the favor by advising him against Dinky's risky venture.

In keeping with his idiosyncratic personality, the designer-contractor had set up store in an unfashionable neighborhood best known for its pawnshops, bail-bond offices, and check-cashing emporia, above a Korean restaurant that had been closed twice by the health department and that couldn't be found in any guide endorsed by the local Asian community. The baseboards were studded with dead phone jacks inherited from an extinct bookmaking operation and the windows were painted over with stylized renditions of imperial palaces, parks, and gardens, as much to blot out views of the surrounding blight as to advertise Kalishnikov's vaunted heritage. The furnishings and décor were luxurious: silk wall coverings, gilded sconces, Turkish rugs, shelves of Morocco-bound books with Cyrillic characters stamped in gold on the spines, velvet-upholstered chairs and sofas, and a great slab of mahogany desk carved with eagles, lions, gryphons, and wicked-looking cherubim that might have been transported directly from Catherine the Great's study in St. Petersburg. Photos of some of the movie meccas the proprietor had designed hung in brushed-steel frames on every wall. Considering the neighborhood, the security system would be the envy of the Federal Reserve.

Kalishnikov could always be expected to adorn himself on

the scale of this habitat. Part of the fun of making an appointment with him was anticipating what over-the-top outfit he'd laid out for himself this time. His silk-lined capes, plush broad-brimmed fedoras, fencing costumes—on some occasions even kilts and a tam-o'-shanter decorated with an Ostrich plume—spoke of a separate building maintained just for wardrobe storage.

This time was different—and so much the opposite extreme that Valentino could only assume that it was further evidence yet of his unconventional nature. He was stretched out on a divan with a gracefully curved headrest, wearing an old brown cardigan pilled all over, baggy poplin slacks, and slippers run down at the heels and nearly worn through at the toes.

He did not rise to greet his visitor, which was unlike him. Instead he raised a smeared tumbler in a sort of toast. A half-full bottle with a Russian bear on the label stood on the floor within his reach.

Vodka—distilled either forty years ago or last Monday—was the choice of drinkers on the sly, under the delusion that it had no odor; the fumes of pure grain alcohol stung Valentino's nostrils on entrance. That accounted for the rosacean stain on the maestro's patrician cheeks.

"Enter, my friend! Drink! There is more where this came from. A friend in Vladivostok sends me a case every Twelfth Night from a secret store in a former fallout shelter. I built him a private theater modeled after the Winter Palace, where he screens *Potemkin* on the anniversary of the October Revolution. A cretin; but he is in possession of more rubles than the second Alexander. And I am a whore who peddles his wares in Gorky Park at a kopeck a pop."

Valentino had seen him tipsy only once, at the party to celebrate The Oracle's completion. That time, too, his speech had been slathered with Russian dressing; but he had not been half

so sodden then. A stub of cigarette smoldered dangerously close
to the tender skin between his fingers.

"It's a little early for me." Valentino shut the door behind him.

"For myself, not so much. In Moscow, the sun is well below
the minarets of St. Basil's."

The atmosphere was becoming far too Slavic for the visitor.
He perched on the edge of a velour chair.

"What did you wish to see me about?"

"You are a detective, yes?"

Dear God.

"Of film. My business cards are clear on that. I don't run
around dusting for fingerprints and breaking alibis."

"But you have experience in locating things, yes? People
also?"

"Information sources, integral to the business of locating and
authenticating certain film properties. *Films*," he emphasized.
The old unassimilated immigrant was about to ask him to track
down some obscure relative in the steppes.

"People! *Da!*" He'd filtered out qualifiers. "I wish you to find
the party who is blackmailing me."

Valentino had already been pursing his mouth to say no. He
felt his face freeze in that position.

Kalishnikov closed one eye and lifted one corner of his
mouth, looking for all the world like Shylock. Using American
idioms always made him appear naughty. "This is the word, is
it not? Blackmail? The unlawful practice of attempting to profit
from threatening to reveal a person's past indiscretions? I see it
on the *Criminal Minds*, the Law and the Order."

"It is the word, yes. Um, what secret does this person claim
to know that would enable him to extort money from you?"

Kalishnikov stroked his upper lip as if there were a moustache there, swirled the non-existent ice in his glass (a few
lozenge-shaped chunks floated in a bowl of water next to the

bottle), drained it, and swallowed, his prominent Adam's apple sliding up and down behind crêpy skin. Extricating the smoldering butt from between his fingers, he dropped it in the glass, where it hissed, then leaned over and thumped the empty vessel on the floor with a thump; sighed, said, with no trace of his usual accent:

"Well, to begin with, it would appear that I am not Russian."

5

VALENTINO TOOK A slow gaze around the room, composing himself. It was like sitting inside a Fabergé egg.

"What's in that bottle, Leo?" He'd never addressed the man by his Christian name before.

"I'm not hallucinating." The accent was as gone as if it had never existed; but then, it came and went on a regular basis. "When I was nine or ten, my mother told me her grandmother came over from Minsk to flee a pogrom. Although I never investigated the claim, I became interested in things Russian, and immersed myself in its history and culture. I was a sickly child, with no friends except the books I read. Later, I spent my allowance on a mail-order course in the language. I regret to say the results were indifferent." Here, he lapsed into the eastern guttural; after that he drifted in and out. "When I came to California with a degree in architecture and interior design, I found myself with many competitors. Some of the most successful, I was soon to notice, assumed characteristics I sensed were not natural to them. It would surprise you to learn how many closet heterosexuals there are in my profession." He turned on his side to offer Valentino the full force of his leer; then settled back with a slicing gesture of his hand. "That pose had gone stale long before I arrived, and in any case it was unsavory and bigoted.

"I struggled," he continued, "working odd drafting jobs for third-rate housing developers, churning out cookie-cutter blue-prints for phony ranch houses, fake Tudors, cheap stuccos, ersatz Cape Cods, lop-sided Bauhauses, and pretentious McMansions, inspecting dusty building sites until I woke up in the middle of the night with air-hammers pounding in my head. I was fired many times, first for not reporting to work, then for insubor-dination, and finally for breaking my employer's nose with a T-square; those were the times when I didn't quit in the middle of a project. In the building trade, I've been black-listed more often than a hard-core Stalinist in old Hollywood. Which brings me to my two patron saints, Mikhail Gorbachev and Ronald Reagan."

His listener remained silent. He was beginning to have a glimmer of where this filibuster was headed.

"My friend, you are too young to know how it felt to wake up one morning and hear on the radio that the Communist Party had been outlawed in Russia. The Berlin Wall had fallen, and soon after the Soviet Union, and the Cold War was at an end. History plays on what you industry insiders refer to as a continuous loop. I had read of the former grand dukes, grand duchesses, counts, countesses, and boyars who had swarmed into this country after the Bolsheviks took over; penniless as they were, having been forced in their haste to abandon their wealth, they were treated by republican Americans as if they still belonged to an elite class; the mystique prevailed. It oc-curred to me that history was repeating itself. While I knew I would make no leeway by pretensions to royalty, I decided that a romantic refugee might warrant closer inspection by a hiring agent than an out-of-work architect from Nebraska; and as it turned out, I was right. I traded my one-and-only business suit for an opera cloak, leotard, and wool-felt Borsalino—all in black, except for the leopard-skin hatband—waltzed in as if I were the director of the North American tour of the Ballet *Russe*, and was appointed immediately to assist the company's head architect." The eye closed again, more slowly than before, and the accent returned. "I am of the personal opinion that the weekend I spent at a local revival house sitting through three showings of *Doctor Zhivago*, playing close attention to Omar Sharif's tonal inflections, were what turned the tide."

"You're from Nebraska?"

"The climate is not dissimilar."

"So your name's not Kalishnikov."

"I borrowed the surname from the Soviet Army's manual of arms; changing the spelling slightly, to turn aside copyright issues."

Sensory overload prevented Valentino from dwelling upon his host's concern of opening himself to a civil suit by a fire-arms manufacturer as opposed to being exposed as an imposter. "How much Russian do you speak?"

"Enough to say hail and farewell and order borscht in a coffee house. When I cannot avoid an encounter with a native, I ask that the conversation be conducted in English, so that I may improve my grasp of the language. I found this ruse to be so successful it astonished me. It emboldened me to consider I was not alone in my subterfuge. Scratch the hide of any California Cossack and you might expect to find a Yankee underneath."

"You're a total fraud?"

Crimson stained further the old man's already flushed features. "I am not even a tenth part of one. I've risen to my present august level through genius alone. That, you cannot falsify. My friend, can you in good conscience condemn a man in this community for applying artistic touches to his background?"

"You're right, of course. The Oracle alone is proof I can't. But since Southern California is more tolerant of self-dramatization than most places, I don't see what harm the truth could do. Your blackmailer has no ammunition."

"It is an intolerable embarrassment."

"You're forgetting this is Hollywood: Land of plastic palms, painted sunsets, false fronts, capped teeth, nose jobs, and publicity machines. Anything that appears genuine is automatically suspect."

"That privilege is restricted to the film colony. I am only marginally connected."

But Valentino was ready for that one. "So was Mike Romanoff."

Kalishnikov paused in the midst of refilling his glass. "I know this name."

"He was a con man who posed as the son of Czar Nicholas, passing bad checks all over town during the Great Depression. He served time in prison and was deported twice. He came back and founded a restaurant that was the toast of Hollywood for decades. By then everyone knew he was a phony, but he continued to insist he was a member of the imperial family until the end of his life. His is one of the town's greatest success stories; and he was a crook. There's nothing illegal about using a trick name and history for self-advertisement. It's no worse than exaggerating your work experience on a job application. Being outed could be even more of a career boost than the fairy tale you invented."

"I was vaguely familiar with the story of this man Romanoff. His story may have played a part in my decision." The pseudo-Russian made a shrug worthy of Mischa Auer. "After all these years, you see, it is difficult to determine where the charade leaves off and the truth begins. At all events, attitudes have changed since his time. Also his legal entanglements were of a trivial nature."

"If you consider a prison sentence trivial—"

"Which I do. I have not been forthcoming with you, my friend; there is more at stake in this matter than personal humiliation. A cheat, a swindler, a bigamist, even a man who has attempted armed robbery may conceivably outlast the stigma of his past, rejoin society, and climb to the heights. What the authorities call a 'class-A felon,' *nyet!*"

While Valentino was attempting to digest that last sentence, his host foraged inside his ratty sweater, snapped open a fold of dirty-looking paper, and passed it across to him.

A much more youthful, but by no means unrecognizable likeness of the designer-contractor appeared in a photograph reproduced muddily by a photocopier in need of service, above two half-columns of print with an Omaha, Neb. dateline under the heading:

MURDER SUSPECT VANISHES
Police in 4 States Join Manhunt

6

HE COULD HEAR Broadhead as if he were physically present: *"What are you, a magnet for murder?"*

It would appear to be the case. Nothing seemed so far removed from a homicide investigation as an academy of higher learning; especially Valentino's chosen field. Such violent deaths as were meant to concern him had taken place a world away, and in mummery. When the director yelled "Cut!" all the corpses got up and went back to their trailers or the studio commissary. But with obnoxious frequency, when the archivist began an expedition into cinema history, he found himself face-to-face with a capital crime.

"You're wanted for murder?"

Kalishnikov made a Slavic gesture of dismissal.

"It was a case of mistaken identity. I was questioned in connection with a fatal love triangle in which a man confronted his wife's lover, who killed him. It seemed I bore some resemblance to the perpetrator. Eventually the man responsible confessed and I was no longer a suspect."

"According to this you fled the interview."

"The detective assigned to the case took an instant dislike to me. I was young and easily intimidated. I knew the wife—casually, I assure you, I am the precise opposite of a satyr—and I could offer no proof that I was elsewhere when the crime was committed; I was convinced the man would frame me and bring a convenient close to the investigation. I excused myself to use the bathroom—the questioning took place in my home—but I did not trouble myself to explain that the bathroom I had in mind was in another state."

"But you knew you were innocent. You should have stood your ground."

"Perhaps. However, the fact that the item you hold in your hand was issued to the press is proof that the detective was after my scalp. I cannot say that, given the same circumstances, I would not do now as I did then."

Valentino looked again at the clipping. "Someone blacked out your name with a marker."

"That was I. Forgive me the conceit. I am baring my soul, but only to a point; allow me to cling to some shred of privacy."

"How did this come to you?"

"By fax, anonymous and untraceable, last week. Whoever sent it is some kind of bloodhound. The newspaper in which it appeared went out of business many years ago."

"What is he—or she—demanding in return for silence?"

"That shoe has not yet dropped. That scrap of paper is all I have received."

"It could be just a prank. I'd ignore it. You've been cleared, so what's the harm in going public, apart from a little embarrassment?"

"Had this taken place a few years ago, I would agree; but the phantom of sexual misbehavior haunts the incident. Careers have been lost in this industry, in some cases merely because the suspicion was raised."

Valentino returned the sheet. "This is way outside my area, Leo. You should go to the police."

"I may as well ignore this warning, and let the chips fall. The result would be the same: exposure and ruin."

"I'd take my chances. It isn't even blackmail until you receive a demand, which may never happen. Someone you don't know, who's jealous of your success, may just be out to needle you."

"I sense it is more than that. You must trust me on this."

"Can you think of anyone who knows you're the person in that article?"

"No one. Well, there is my daughter."

The blows just kept coming. How, in the midst of mastering the science of architecture, constructing an entirely fictitious identity, and fleeing persecution, had this man managed to father a child? The answer came before he could ask.

"I had a wife, who sued me for desertion after I left. In that time she gave birth. She was kind enough to send me a picture along with the divorce papers." He rolled over on one hip, produced a crocodile billfold, and passed over the snapshot he'd fished out. A slightly heavyset woman with a grave, pretty face held a chubby infant wrapped in a pink blanket. Valentino gave it back.

"It may surprise you to learn that I am not a selfish man. I sent my former wife a check every month for fifteen years. When I learned of her death, I sent another to my daughter, under her mother's maiden name. She went back to it after the divorce."

This time he searched inside his sweater for several moments, then produced a folded and dirty envelope. A yellow sticker was attached, announcing that the recipient, Carla Schmeisser, had moved and left no forwarding address. The original Omaha address was legible, as was the ten-year-old postmark. "It would pain me to think that my own flesh would choose to make me a victim," he said, "but there is no accounting for the human condition. At all events she may know something. Perhaps she can be traced."

Valentino started to give it back.

Kalishnikov threw up his hands, spilling vodka on himself and the divan. "If you refuse me, I am lost!"

"I wish I could help."

"What can I do that will entice you, if friendship is not sufficient?"

His guest fell silent; not for lack of an answer, but because it meant both exploiting a fellow creature in distress and committing himself once again to an enterprise best left to a real detective. If only the man hadn't brought up friendship! Valentino took a deep breath and told him Dinky Schwartz's scheme and why Kalishnikov's participation was needed.

The theater designer set his glass on the floor and sat straight up. Suddenly he seemed no longer to be in a state of inebriation.

"I am familiar with this phenomenon, this very American practice of dining, taking amusement, and even attending funerals, without leaving one's automobile. I should welcome the opportunity to apply my considerable talents to such an enterprise. When can we visit this deserted arena—or should I say blank canvas?"

THIRTY MINUTES LATER, Kalishnikov emerged from seclusion, dressed entirely in black: Ankle-length cassock, stout lace-up boots, ebony stick with an onyx knob, and a shovel hat. All hail the Grand Inquisitor! Reassuringly, his complexion had reverted to its characteristic polished alabaster and his eyes were as clear and bright as blue marbles.

"Do me a favor," Valentino said. "Don't give me the name of your tailor."

Kalishnikov smiled, taking this as a compliment. "I have an arrangement with the various studio wardrobe departments; they lend me some of their choicest items, and I provide advice to their art directors, waiving my fee." He brandished his stick. "Lay on, MacDuff: to the country of the barbarians."

"Try not to say that out loud. Many of my customers come from there."

The passenger accommodated his disproportionately long legs to the interior of the foreign compact and they headed out to the Valley.

Schwartz, who'd agreed over the phone to meet them at the defunct drive-in, had a blueprint-reader's gift for accurate directions. Despite Southern California traffic, they arrived in acceptably short order in front of a twenty-acre parcel at the end of a string of strip malls, housing developments, convenience stores, and auto dealerships. The company's sign decorated the obligatory ten-foot board fence, with smaller cardboard signs posted at regular intervals warning the public to keep out. Valentino's college buddy stood inside the open gate, decked out in gray coveralls and a yellow hard hat. The driver pulled onto a gravel apron separating the fence from the street, next to Schwartz's floating continent of a truck.

Alighting, he pointed at the headgear. "Do we get helmets?"

"Not necessary. Nothing's doing yet. I put it on whenever I visit a site; shifts me into high gear."

Kalishnikov clucked his tongue. "A pity. I should admire to have added it to my collection."

Introductions were made. Schwartz, a native of the Golden State, where the unconventional was the norm, showed no surprise at the "Russian's" outfit. He appeared to modify the bone-crushing grip he'd given Valentino when shaking the other's hand; a concession, perhaps, to the man's age. In any case the designer betrayed no discomfort.

"Let's get to the damage report." Schwartz stood aside and they stepped past him.

The place was as Valentino had pictured, a vast expanse of sun-bleached asphalt with clumps of oat grass growing up through the cracks, faded yellow lines parsing out the parking spaces, some with the aluminum posts that had once borne portable speakers leaning at Krazy Kat angles, most naked of same; a dilapidated stucco building the size of a bare-bones highway rest stop, its windows blanked out with plywood, spray-painted with the inevitable graffiti—presumably the concession area; and the ruined sacred altar of a forty-foot screen, now just a steel frame stripped of its fabric, pitted with rust and canted from its original rectangle into a drunken trapezoid. Tumbleweeds frolicked about; a bit of commentary added in post-production. Some thrifty owner had used an old sign to close a gap in the fence that enclosed the lot: It offered roast peanuts for sale at a nickel a bag. Flaked pink script on a field of sea-green described an ascending arc above the entrance, ending in a five-pointed star:

THE COMET

"Splendidly prophetic!" Kalishnikov pronounced. "A spectacle born of heaven, extinguished in the blink of an eye."

"Well, even Halley's comes back every seventy-five years," said Schwartz.

Valentino said, "It may take this one that long."

Kalishnikov appeared not to have heard him. Galvanized, he wandered the entire space, looking up at the sky, down at the ground, and all around the perimeter, pausing sometimes to form a square with his hands and peer through it in the time-honored attitude of an auteur visualizing a location as it would photograph; once even lowering himself to his knees and measuring the width of a parking space with his ebony stick. Gone was the old man wallowing in self-pity in his overdecorated garret. Here was the veteran designer of public and private theaters who'd explored The Oracle for the first time, seeing not piles of broken plaster, tattered and stained upholstery, burst pipes, and dangerous wiring, but the fabulous shrine as it once had been and would be again.

At length he rose, brushed dirt from his cassock, and rejoined the others, dusting off his palms. "I am unschooled in this area," he said, "but it would seem to me that one could admit many more customers into this space than when last it was in operation. One could crowd two automobiles like Mr. Valentino's charming imported conveyance in a space formerly occupied by a DeSoto or a Studebaker."

Schwartz smacked the top of his hard hat. "Bingo! We could restrict two full rows to compacts and squeeze a fleet of Hummers and Land Rovers into the others." He rubbed his hands. "This mean we're good to go?"

"'Good to go.'" Kalishnikov beamed. "I never tire of the American vernacular when it comes to accomplishing the impossible." He was back in full Russian mode; even his accent was comic-opera incarnate.

Valentino's heart sank. Secretly, he'd hoped the man would turn down the project; but genius and common sense were hardly opposite sides of the same coin.

The archivist was sure to fail in what he'd been asked to do, or worse; he might succeed. What then? How well did he know, really, Leo Kalishnikov? In the course of one afternoon, everything he *assumed* he knew—his nationality, his lack of family, his freedom from complication apart from pure artistry—had turned out to be a lie. His claim of innocence had been rushed, his claim that he'd been cleared of the charge he'd left home to escape unsatisfactory; even suspect. What if Valentino had agreed to serve as an accessory to murder?

7

THEY ADJOURNED TO the old concession stand, gutted now of its popcorn popper, corn dog rotisseries, ice cream freezer, cotton candy maker, and soda fountain, and refurnished with a chipboard desk and folding metal chairs; but haunted still by the ghosts of hot grease, melted butter, and spun sugar, grown stale now but still as potent as a half-remembered tune playing over and over in one's head. An industrial-size Thermos stood on the desk, all gleaming stainless steel; it looked like a cold-war missile. Without bothering to ask his guests if they wanted refreshment, Dinky Schwartz poured iced tea into three red Solo cups. Schwartz raised his. "Shall we toast our new enterprise?"

"Not just yet," Valentino said. "We haven't heard what Leo has to say."

Russian or not, the designer presented the inscrutable expression of Politburo members on a reviewing stand.

"Challenges abound," he said after a moment. "There are four major freeways within earshot, a situation that did not exist when the Comet was, shall we say, at its zenith. I fear that in order to drown out the bellow of horns, shriek of brakes, and din of collisions, you must crank up the sound system so high, the bursting of collective eardrums will render the solution moot."

Schwartz smiled.

"I've already discussed arrangements with the Department of Transportation. Their engineers built the sound-retaining walls in the suburbs near LAX, Oakland, and San Diego; they'll fence in the whole shebang for a fee that's snug inside the budget. Those baffles were designed to deaden the scream of jet engines, so traffic noise is no sweat. Guys, a visit to the Comet will be as peaceful as a night in a home theater."

"Ah, but the experience must be superior! Else why venture from the comfort of one's furnished basement?"

"Isn't that the point? Escape means movement; your old Berlin Wall is proof of that."

But the spectre of the Iron Curtain seemed lost on Kalishnikov. At times, a show of stony resolve on the old man's part meant he was in doubt; at others it was simply a barricade he erected between himself and the world while he focused on the future. Fraud he may be in some things, but not when it came to his work. Perhaps he was finding the challenges of this project beyond the price of the reward. Valentino felt a ray of hope. He might get out of this yet, without bruising any friendships.

"Zoning may be an insurmountable problem," he said, trying not to sound eager. "This area is heavily residential. Even if the board were inclined to issue a variance, you'd need the permission of all the local homeowners. That's like herding cats."

But Dinky's rapture was impregnable. "Val, don't forget you're talking to a pro. All you and Mr. K. have to worry about is the design. Leave the bureaucrats to me."

Kalishnikov spoke before Valentino could turn to him. His words chilled.

"If what you say is so, I see no reason why this project cannot proceed. Of course, I am only a contract worker, and can have no role in any partnership. I leave the decision to those better qualified."

He was passing the buck; and in that moment Valentino knew he was sold—and that he himself was on the hook, unless he managed to spit it out. It was either jeopardize two friendships he valued or consent to bury himself under a load of debt he could never hope to dig out of.

He scoured his brain for a third option; some example negative enough to reverse the course of the conversation.

Schwartz drew a fold of stiff paper from his coveralls. "I've taken the liberty." He passed it across the Valentino. "Go over it with your lawyer, and if he approves, we can iron out the rest of the details. Welcome aboard, partner!"

Valentino opened it carefully, as if a spider might leap out. His gaze slid uncomprehendingly down the inventory of quaint Old World terminology ("whereas," heretofore," etc.) and came with a sudden stop on bold print:

ADVANCE DUE ON SIGNING:

$250,000 (Two Hundred Fifty Thousand Dollars)

8

THIS WAS IT. The figure was ten times the population of his Indiana hometown.

The decision, of course, was no less obvious than it had been all along. He drew in what was likely the last breath of fresh air in the San Fernando Valley and let it out.

"Dink—"

Kalishnikov interrupted. "A moment of privacy, perhaps, Mr. Schwartz?"

"Sure. I've been wanting to take some measurements since you mentioned that parking idea." He snatched up a unicycle-like contraption that had been leaning in a corner and let himself out, pushing the door shut behind him.

The Russian (for Valentino would always think of him as such) lifted off his ecclesiastical hat, ceremoniously with both hands, and deposited it on the desk. He remained in character. "You have doubts, my friend. It is the money, no?"

"It is the money, yes. When I finish paying off the bathroom renovation at the Oracle, I'll be out of debt for the first time in ten years. The theater's a success so far, but only a fool would count on lightning striking twice, especially on anything as iffy as a drive-in movie in the age of streaming and YouTube. I only strung along on Dinky's deal this far because he's an old friend and I didn't want to dash his hopes."

"Strung along, or strung him along? There is a difference."

The artist's practical side shocked him into nodding.

"You're right. My stomach's been in knots ever since he sprang this on me. The truth is I was counting on you to shoot down the idea so I wouldn't have to."

Kalishnikov shook his head; a gesture most expressive when practiced in the eastern European fashion, like a bull under attack by gnats.

"This is not you. I saw the glitter in your eye when we were discussing practical measures; something I have not seen since you and I wandered the aisles in architectural outlets, fondling brass knobs and plaster statuary. We stumbled together on that statue of winged Pegasus that had migrated from the foot of the Oracle's grand staircase to the San Fernando Valley; that glitter was a thing aflame." He held up an index finger sporting a popish ring with a stone the size of a robin's egg. "The spirit is willing, but the flesh is busted flat. In such times it is better to listen to the spirit."

Busted flat: The brief shift to American slang brought Valentino up short.

"And for every hour I spent shopping for gewgaws I spent two pleading my case in banks and credit unions throughout Greater Los Angeles. None of the loan officers I met with asked me for spirit as collateral."

"I am neither a bank nor a credit union, but I have not done badly since I came to this—California," *this country*: Kalishnikov had corrected himself in mid-stride. "And I would not dream of taking possession of your spirit. That is the very thing that persuaded me to collaborate with you in the first place.

These overnight millionaires, these dot-com-poops who wish merely to seduce investors with a movie night in their base-ments, pah! They are not simpatico, like you and me. I spit on their wallets!" He proceeded to illustrate that by a dry expecto-ration at the floor between his feet.

Valentino felt the same guilty pleasure that came with a shot at a lost film pursued by competitors for decades; also the fear of unintended consequences. "If you're offering me a loan—"

The speech that followed was pure Omaha, combined with an upheld palm.

"Whoa! I'm not Bill Gates. You've been no more dishonest than Schwartz; much less so. Your old pal is a chiseler. He thinks because you got some press over a couple of choice acquisitions, you're rich enough to take pressure off his bank account."

"He's not a crook! How can you say that on ten minutes' ac-quaintance?"

"Those black-and-white films you love have made you see the world in just those colors. All business is conducted in various tones of gray. Every great success story was written on some sucker's back. Listen to me!"

Strong fingers closed on Valentino's arm; Dinky needn't have taken mercy on the old man, whose voice sank to a harsh and earnest whisper, and his vocabulary to the level of Wall Street.

"No one asks for exactly as much as he needs," he went on. "The richer you are, the steeper the pitch. I can manage a hundred grand, and if the enterprise succeeds, we'll split the take. Seventy-thirty, in my favor; as I said, I am not Bill Gates, but nor am I Mother Teresa. If there is no profit, I can deduct the loss and enter a less unreasonable tax bracket. I would be a silent investor, with no agenda but the satisfaction that comes from a victory over the infidels."

"I don't see how I merit thirty percent. I'm putting up nothing."

Abruptly the Russian-English patois reasserted itself. Valentino wondered if he was even aware of the shifts back and forth.

"Your investment is passion. It is the intangible that cannot be discounted. It is what was missing from every bold venture that broke up on the rocks, from the Edsel to the Bay of Pigs. We are friends, are we not? Brothers in the ongoing revolution against the bourgeoisie. This paper"—he tore the contract from Valentino's hands and smacked it with his knuckles—"is just the opening of *The 1812 Overture*. It builds and builds to the booming of the guns; but you need not foot the bill for the powder and shot. Counter with an offer of a hundred, and do not agree to anything more than one-fifty."

Valentino grasped only the gist of this lecture on twenty-first-century economics. "I expected you only to offer your services as a designer in return for helping you out with your—your problem. I never intended to suck you into so risky a proposition."

"Philanthropy is for those with a guilty conscience. I am an entrepreneur. In return I ask that you locate my daughter, and should she prove not to be my blackmailer, that you locate the individual who is, and if possible spare me the scarlet stain of murder." Kalishnikov's grin was as broad as the Volga River, and as devious as Rasputin. "We are comrades, yes? I think yes. Free me from my past; this is all I ask."

"That's *all*?"

"It is a great deal to expect; but I would not do so had I not seen you raise Atlantis from the deep and solve the riddle of the dead leopard on Mount Kilimanjaro. You are what the visitors to the first Peter's court referred to as *savant*. You must not waste this gift, lest it atrophy."

"But—"

The old man showed a set of teeth convincingly of Soviet manufacture: White lead soldered over what was likely inferior steel. "Ask your old friend to rejoin us. He's had time by now to measure the entire Los Angeles watershed."

AS ALWAYS WHEN he paid more attention to his thoughts than the road, Valentino found himself back at Harriet's; his Korean compact horse knew the way to carry the sleigh. She was curled up on the couch, barefoot and in cutoffs and a T-shirt that read STOLEN FROM SING SING PENITENTIARY—an aggressively non-departmental uniform—reading a paperback mystery. She tossed it aside when he came through the door.

"I don't so much mind a cat catching a murderer as the amateur detective who owns the flea-bitten beast," she said. "Why do these scribblers insist on making their heroines such ninnies? They do more damage to women's rights than an army of good-ole-boy hillbillies. I swear my department supervisor bases all his assignments on the latest entry in the *Fast and Furry-ous* line."

He picked it up and looked at the back. "That's a lot to expect for seven dollars and ninety-nine cents."

"Adjusted for inflation, that comes to forty pieces of silver."

"Why take it so personally? You're always telling me you forensics experts aren't police officers. I locked out all the CSIs because you toss and turn all night over the inaccuracies."

She drew her brows into a knife-line crease. "Why do you look like you just traded your 401(k) for a handful of magic beans?"

"How'd we get from Rita Mae Brown to Mother Goose?"

"This isn't Brown. She at least has wit. It's one of her faded clones, the Brownlets; who are witless." Her forehead smoothed out. "You bought something."

He knew her face well enough to take the accusatory-sounding phrase as a warm invitation. Their incomes were separate. Money was one thing they never quarreled about.

He grinned. "Ever make out at a drive-in movie?"

9

HARRIET'S FIRST REMARK after he'd finished threw him.

"Someone came looking for you. He went to your office first. Ruth told him you might try here or at the Oracle. She's inconsistent, isn't she? Guards the film preservation department like the three-headed Hydra, but when it comes to someone's private life she's Rona Barrett."

He'd told her about the arrangement with Dinky Schwartz and Leo Kalishnikov's involvement, but left out his own agreement to look into his extortion complaint, letting her think the theater designer's interest was purely that of a fellow enthusiast. His personal troubles weren't public property. Valentino had expected some expression of disapproval, if only because she cared about him and wouldn't want to see him immerse himself in another morass; and of course there was the memory of dates canceled, memorable anniversaries forgotten, and everything else that wedged itself between romantic involvement and pressing matters from outside.

Regrettably (later, in retrospect), his reaction was based on curiosity. He was, after all, a seeker of information, if not precisely the detective he advertised himself to be on his business cards.

"Who was it? Did he say what he wanted?"

"You're even less of a cop than you say I am. You can't conduct an interrogation with more than one question at a time and expect an answer you can work with. He didn't leave his name and wouldn't discuss his business with me. Here." She gave him a card on heavy professional stock she took from a slacks pocket. It was blank except for a telephone number handwritten in blocky numerals. The prefix, 308, meant nothing to him.

"What did he look like?"

"Now we're making progress in the field of investigation. If I were a contestant on the old *What's My Line?*—which was canceled when my parents were in rompers—and had to guess, I'd say he's a dirt farmer."

"Is there any other kind?"

"Well, there's hydroponics, but he didn't fit that mold. Face burned red from wind or sun or both, sloping shoulders, calluses on his calluses, rusty black suit, clodhoppers on his feet, broad-brimmed felt hat clutched in front of him like Gary Cooper, some kind of Midwestern drawl: Ohio, maybe, or Wisconsin, North Dakota, maybe—"

"Nebraska?" He felt a chill just saying it.

"Could be. One of those places whose residents think they speak without an accent, like yours."

"I don't have an accent."

"What I said. If I didn't know you as well as I do, I'd suspect you'd answered an advertisement trying to lure you into some kind of cult. You know, one of those deals where you hoe somebody else's soybean field sixteen hours a day in return for eternal life and a permanent courtside seat in a game between the Yahweh Yahoos and the Beelzebub Bobcats."

"Any chance he's a policeman?"

She raised her brows. "What have you done now—besides plunging into a six-figure business arrangement like you were buying a toothbrush?"

"Nothing." *Yet.* "So?"

"Could be. I mean, if I were a casting director and needed someone to play a country constable who covers his beat aboard a mule."

"No kidding, cops really call it a beat?"

"Of course not. I'm translating for the contemporarily challenged."

He abandoned banter; his heart hadn't really been in it. "How about a crook?"

"No comment. They come in all varieties. Val, is there something I should know about?"

"If I knew myself I'd tell you. Anonymous strangers who know where I work and live and show up unannounced make me nervous, that's all." He changed the subject. "I have some work to clear up back at the office. Do you want to go out to dinner later?"

"Are you sure you can afford it?" She retrieved her novel with a smirk.

THE BULBOUS OLD CRT monitor on his desk looked like a prop from *Star Wars*. He fired it up and surfed for the number on the card Harriet had given him. It got no results, but Google identified the 308 exchange.

It didn't have to be significant. If it was a cell number, it could have been ordered from anywhere. And if Leo Kalishnikov could claim the place as his home state, so could some two million others. Whatever his mysterious visitor wanted, it didn't have to have anything to do with something that had happened many years ago in Nebraska.

Ruth came in without knocking. Her suspiciously black hair, varnished like ebony furniture, steel-rimmed spectacles, and long, clawlike, blood-red nails, but most of all her very presence, brought the temperature down several degrees in any room she entered.

"You blasted past my station like an anti-ballistic missile. I didn't get the chance to give you this." She flung one of her bowdlerized memo sheets down on the desk, pivoted on her natural axis, and clacked out on platform heels. She'd come to Hollywood during its Golden Age intending to knock Rita Hayworth off her perch and had wound up a generation later directing traffic for the UCLA Film and TV Preservation Department—an arm of the educational institution she considered worthless. She'd have been forcibly retired years ago if she weren't as icily efficient as an Enigma machine; and if the regents weren't intimidated by her down to the man.

Valentino glanced down at the scrap of paper, saw *Cleopatra*, grimaced, and flung it into the circular file without another glance. He had a premonition that this particular pest would be more difficult to exterminate than most.

The thing forgotten, at least for the time being, he disinterred Kalishnikov's creased and smudged envelope from his pocket and read the name it had been addressed to, and which the United States Postal Service had been unable to locate:

Carla Schmeisser.

The film archivist gave vent to a snort, as unexpected and involuntary as a hiccup. The surname, reportedly her mother's maiden name, belonged to an automatic weapon, and unlike Kalishnikov, was spelled correctly. He wondered if this was what had inspired the old humbug's *nom du guerre*.

He ran a search for the name, but again came up empty (except for a large number of Schmeissers with no apparent connection to Nebraska). As Broadhead was fond of pointing out, the grid was not omniscient, or it would not insist that whales and dolphins swam in the fresh water of the Great Lakes. She might be living under a different name, possibly since before her father had sent the check that was never cashed—married, possibly, and living as Mrs. Smith or Jones or Brown or Venus Aquarius. Any of those circumstances would explain the inability of the mighty U.S. Postal Service to track her down.

All this had taken place years ago. The woman might be dead. Even if not, there was absolutely no evidence she had anything to do with the blackmail attempt.

And so the amateur sleuth had managed to stall at the very beginning of a simple missing-persons investigation. What had Leo been thinking when he came to him with it? And what had Valentino been thinking when he agreed to take it on?

To fail meant the loss of his silent (paying!) partner and the end of The Comet; also of his friendship with Dinky Schwartz.

Unacceptable.

And just possibly unnecessary.

Valentino had built his reputation not on state-of-the-art technology, but by mining the non-digital past, and by relying on his instincts. He picked up the card the stranger had left with Harriet and, like every detective he admired on the old silver screen, lifted the receiver off the landline and dialed the number.

10

THE LINE PURRED five times and then a recording came on asking him to wait for the tone. It was that sterile female voice that came with voice mail and revealed nothing about the user. Valentino hung up without leaving a message. His mystery man was persistent, and would call back after checking his records.

He glanced at the old-school clock on the wall, a wheezing electric relic from the building's origins as the university heating plant. The Los Angeles Public Library was open, and his friendship with Dinky Schwartz was at least worth an hour's research into the history of drive-in movies.

At the reception desk he told Ruth where he could be reached. She replied without looking up from her keyboard. "In and out, out and in. Beatniks!"

The library was in the process of converting its microfilm records to digital. Fortunately, it had started with the earliest newspapers on file: Spanish-language journals dating back to the old *Alcalde* of Zorro legend. It would be weeks before the project entered the twentieth century.

The sprawling facility was lit up like a 7-Eleven and furnished with steel shelves built low enough to see over into the next aisle, minimizing claustrophobia. It smelled of floor wax and glued bindings. During the transition to e-file, the documents on microfilm had been moved into the section previously assigned to out-of-town telephone directories.

Valentino found the shelves he wanted sequestered in a corner near the fire exit. Small square black cardboard boxes lined the shelves, labeled with dates belonging to back issues of the *L.A. Times*, *Herald*, and *San Francisco Call*, the old Hearst publication. He gathered up a span from the Truman, Eisenhower, and Kennedy era—it was like pressing a dozen building blocks between his palms—and carried them to a carrel with a viewing machine. He fixed a fishing-reel-size spool of film onto the machine, threaded the end onto the take-up wheel, and became H. G. Wells.

Which was no exaggeration. Second to movies themselves, viewing microfilm was like operating a time machine. Scroll back, say, to the Apollo moon landing, scroll forward to Afghanistan, and you shed years one way or reclaimed them the other, all with a hand on the crank.

It was a simple device, for all its wonder; a lightbulb and a mirror inside a metal box. Hardly an improvement on an old-time magic lantern, but so useful to the student of modern history.

The Comet opened in June 1948, the year Hollywood lost its monopoly on motion-picture theaters and television eclipsed movies in popularity. The studios had to do something to recoup, and they jumped on any new innovation like a drowning man snatching at driftwood: Wide-screen Cinerama, three-D, no novelty was too outlandish to consider. Valentino searched the entertainment sections for more on the subject, resisting the urge to loiter among the advertisements for *Fort Apache*,

Key Largo, and *The Red Shoes*, cramming as for a test. Kyle Broadhead would approve of his student work ethic.

The grand opening leapt out at him like a gimmick in a William Castle film. That early in their history, drive-ins were hot copy, this one in a full-page spread in the *Herald* with a large photo of bulbous automobiles parked in orderly rows like eggs in a carton. *Tarzan and the Mermaids* was frozen in mid-action on the monster screen in the background; he recognized Johnny Weissmuller in his last appearance in the loincloth, scowling at George Zucco, wearing his trademark tarboosh. A color inset featured the shooting-star sign, arcing ever upward in a surge of hope and *hubris*. The headline read:

**SEE THE STARS FROM YOUR CAR, SAYS OWNER OF
"THE COMET"**

There followed six columns of interviews with the owner, ushers, car hops, and starry-eyed customers. It all read suspiciously like free advertising; but probably had not come free at all. The facing page featured a four-color spread promoting the theater, complete with coming attractions and discounts on ladies' night.

The enterprise couldn't have come at a more convenient time. Peacetime audiences were eager to embrace anything new, and with veterans back home and the population exploding, the promised combination of convenience and diversion had convinced the country, if there had been any doubt, that it had won the war.

The *Times* covered the event a week later, in two columns and only a headshot of the owner below the fold on the last page of the section. It was accompanied by an ad of only a quarter-page.

Tobias Winters, thirtyish and pudgy-faced, pale in the flare of the flash, was the bold adventurer behind The Comet. A man ahead of his time, this creature, in turned-up hat brim and baggy suit. In today's world he'd be a computer geek with his glasses taped together and seven figures in the bank.

What had become of him? Had he passed from one success to another? Lived quietly and comfortably on his early profits? Or had he followed the example of Max Fink, the dreamer behind The Oracle, and plunged headlong from the peak of triumph into the depth of disaster, like the shooting star that inspired him?

Sadly, that seemed to be the scenario. The Comet's celebrity dwindled as competition grew from motor-driven pleasure palaces across the continent. In time it was mentioned only routinely, in a list with its rivals as the movement became part of the accepted reality of an America without gasoline rationing, and of course on the advertising pages: *Invasion of the Saucer Men*, *Hot Rods to Hell*, *Bwana Devil*; the fare descended in quality as turnout increased. And then the turnout followed suit.

In 1960, Winters sold his interest to a syndicate of investors, who found too late that the pig they'd bought in a poke was sterile. Malaise had set in: Vietnam, Watergate, the energy crisis, Daylight Savings Time; an hour saved was an hour stolen from the theater of the night.

1972: Los Angeles County levied a stiff fine against The Comet for booking adult features in full view of motorists traveling along I-15; an exposed breast on a screen forty feet wide threatened to create a pile-up. After that, the theater was mentioned only once, when it was shuttered eight years later and its screen and outbuildings condemned. By then a recession had set in, delaying demolition. Total press coverage of the decision came to six inches with no accompanying art. It was the story of The Oracle all over again; and all over again, Valentino had been called upon to come to the rescue.

He rewound the spool, returned it to its box, and just to be thorough got up to comb through the recent newspapers suspended by wooden poles in a rack in the periodicals section. The library had ceased committing back numbers to microfilm when it went digital, so there was nothing on the shelves beyond 2010. He spread out the analog copies on a vacant reading table to leaf through.

Eighteen months ago, the Sunday feature sections of both L.A. papers hailed the renaissance of an American institution, citing the appearance of updated outdoor theaters here and there in Southern California. But there was little of substance in those accounts, only nostalgia leavened with such technological improvements as in-dash access to soundtracks, replacing the window-mounted speakers of the Eisenhower years. Like that article in *Parade*, it was file copy set aside for a slow news day, like a dog playing badminton, and slightly stale. He returned the papers to the rack, knowing little more than he had at the start.

So why did he feel that dangerous thrum of excitement building? He was as much a hopeless case as Dinky Schwartz.

An apologetic voice on the P.A. system alerted the patrons that the library would close in ten minutes. Startled, Valentino confirmed the time on his phone: 8:50 P.M. Once again the past had devoured the present.

It was summer on the Left Coast, and therefore twilight; the ideal time to revisit The Comet at the peak hour of its illustrious past.

11

ONE'S FIRST VISIT to the Valley after a long absence was always a refreshing change of pace; less so the second. Maybe a return to the neighborhood would shock him back to his senses.

The location at that hour, with no magic unfolding on the ruined screen, provided all the charm of prowling through a suburban cellar with a flashlight. A milkwater half-moon smirked through bales of smog at a twenty-acre patch of pulverized asphalt, bats fluttering around the light of the only street lamp in blocks, speaker poles slanting this way and that, tumbleweeds and Marlboro boxes bouncing across the cracked pavement in the wind from Mexico. Valentino slid into a centrally located space and cut his motor. The din of cicadas filled the car. He pictured himself watching *Task Force* with James Cagney, Margaret Wycherly, and Virginia Mayo in *White Heat*; a movie-within-a-movie: Warner Brothers slyly advertising one of its own features within another. It was in just such a place—maybe the actual one?—that Cagney's psychotic gang leader Cody Jarrett had fled to evade a high-speed police car chase. Both films had appeared in 1949, a year after The Comet opened.

Someone rapped on his window.

He jumped in his seat. Cagney was dead, of course; but had his ghost returned to make certain of Jarrett's alibi?

Valentino cranked down the glass. A man in an old-fashioned broad-brimmed hat, rusty black suit, yellowed white shirt fastened at the neck with a string tie, and—when he spoke—a gust of dried corn shocks from someplace like Nebraska—said, "Mr. Valentino? I've been trying to get in touch with you for days. You're as hard to track down as a badger in his hole. That varmint takes a lot of killing, believe you me."

TO THIS PROFESSIONAL academic, "fight or flight" was hardly a matter of choice. He had a sudden panicky urge to start the car and shove the accelerator to the floor, peeling off rubber like a getaway driver fleeing the scene of a botched robbery, shot by a second unit. But thousands of hours of crime movies had warned him that this was invariably met with gunfire, punching a hole through the rear window and whoever was inside the car; usually the most harmless actor in the scene, which described him down to the ground.

He subsided against the back of his seat and wound down the window.

The man was older than anticipated. His face was gray and papery, like newspaper clippings that had been shut up for years in an attic with no exposure to the sun, and his teeth—for he was one of those elderly men who smiled constantly, as if endeavoring to please—were too white and even to have grown in his mouth naturally. Triangles of sagging skin were folded sharply over the edges of his eyelids; Valentino thought of dogeared pages in an old book.

Too old, he thought, for a law enforcement officer. Was there a mandatory retirement age for civilian bounty hunters? Maybe he was a vigilante; a relative or close friend of that dead woman in Omaha, who refused to believe the man who'd confessed to her murder had told the truth, and was pursuing a personal vendetta against Leo Kalishnikov.

Or was he the actual killer? A desperate man determined to eliminate the last witness who could overturn the original verdict and place him on Death Row? Valentino had Philo Vance, Nick and Nora Charles, and Boston Blackie to vouch for such a theory. Had Grote latched onto him as the means to that end? Advanced age did not preclude the ability to kill.

Stall for time.

"Who told you I'd be here?"

"Your secretary said you were going to the library. I got there just as you came out the door, and followed you here. Really, Mr. Valentino, this wouldn't have been necessary if you'd just got back to me. I called and called, and left a message with your lady friend in person."

Called? Valentino knew only about the man's visit to Harriet's.

He played for more time, consulting all his mirrors. "Where's your car?"

"I used Uber. He's gone now; I couldn't afford to pay him to wait. I can't afford a car either. I'll be shank's mare all the way back to my hotel if I can't hitch a ride. That's one of the reasons I wanted to talk to you."

Money.

Blackmail.

He felt a rush of relief. If this were merely the man who was squeezing Kalishnikov, he was unlikely to be a physical threat. Blackmailers don't kill: wasn't that a tenet of the celluloid thriller? He needed to take a break from movies.

"If it's blood money you want," he said, "I'm broke. You should make an arrangement with Leo."

The elderly face contracted into a mass of wrinkles, like Saran Wrap. He was either genuinely flummoxed or a master at faking it.

Valentino grew tired of the game. "Who are you?"

The smile seemed to be a permanent fixture. It wasn't intended to please.

"The name won't make no difference to you, till it comes to signing a check."

The man had been hugging himself on one side, as if he had a pain in his ribs. Now he raised that arm and presented the package he'd been clasping to his hip: A thick manila mailer, torn and grubby, containing something that stretched its seams to bursting. When Valentino reached to accept it, he jerked it back, hugging it to his chest with both hands.

"It's empty, just so you know. I'd of been less whatchallit, *circumspect*, if you'd had the common courtesy to get back to me."

He worked his mouth, evidently to resettle his dentures; then thrust out the package in both hands.

Valentino took it and reached inside, half expecting a snake or some spring-operated device to inject a lethal substance into his hand. (He really had to find another hobby.) Then he felt one of the most reassuring sensations in his career: The solid shape of a two-inch-thick metal canister, suitable for containing a full-size pizza, but more likely something far less ephemeral. With his heart thudding through his wrist, he withdrew a gray steel film can, rusted around the edges, with its contents stenciled across the top, in ink characters nearly as faded as the Dead Sea Scrolls:

CLEOPATRA

10/14/17

Fox Film Corporation

Do Not Remove From Studio

Valentino nearly lost his grip on the can. The container itself, if genuine, was worth thousands to fanatic collectors, who would snatch at even so slight a vestige of one of the Grails of the motion-picture industry. He knew then his folly: He'd mixed up his own ardent pursuer at the UCLA Film and TV Preservation Department with Leo Kalishnikov's tormentor, and the abysmal 1963 *Cleopatra* with legendary screen vamp Theda Bara's magnum opus, considered lost for more than a century.

He unlocked the door on the passenger's side. "Hop in. Have you had supper?"

II

BAKED NEBRASKA

12

THE NEAREST RESTAURANT was a family place: A barnlike building with exposed heating pipes overhead, painted beige to make them recede into the ceiling. Patrons in jeans, sweats, and cutoffs sat around plank tables in Windsor chairs, each group arranged in descending order of age from white-haired patriarchs to tow-headed tots, and business was lively around the great canoe-shaped salad bar in the center of the room. The level of conversation was loud enough, and the pitch sufficiently varied, to discourage eavesdroppers. Valentino and his companion were free to talk.

They seated themselves at one of the smaller tables in a corner with Norman Rockwell prints framed on the walls. When their purple-haired waitress bustled off to fill their orders, the archivist drummed his fingers on the film can in his lap; he'd hardly dared leave it in the car and forbore to bring it into the open.

The man across from him chuckled; it was a dry sound, like two sanding blocks rubbing against each other. "What's the matter? Think that fat kid in the high chair's a spy?"

"I wouldn't rule him out. Whenever something like this comes to light it sends vibes throughout the community." Teddie Goodman, and her deep-pocket benefactor, Mark David Turkus, were particularly attuned to that frequency; but he kept silent about that. For all he knew, his fellow diner was in league with the enemy and this was some kind of trap.

The can was empty, for one thing. He knew what a reel of film weighed and recognized the hollow thump when he tapped the container. The worn quality of the stenciled title on the lid looked authentic, but there were experts who would take care to make it appear so.

Still, the bait was worth sniffing at. If it wasn't a decoy, and had once contained *Cleopatra*, could the prize be far away?

"Before this goes any further," he said—"whatever *this* is—I must tell you I don't do business with anonymous parties. I can't. Hollywood practically wrote the definition of intellectual property. Money could change hands, the, uh, *property*"—he was almost superstitiously reluctant to call it by name—"could be in my possession, and it could turn out I owned nothing at all. What would I tell a judge, if the legal owner of the copyright takes me to court and I'm asked how I came by it? 'Your Honor, it was a chance meeting in an abandoned drive-in movie lot, with a man who refused to identify himself, but who looked and sounded like Grandpa Walton'?"

"Really?" The stranger frowned. "I usually get Sean Connery, without the fruity Scotch accent."

Valentino had nothing to say to that.

At length the old man sighed, took a shabby brown leather wallet from his hip, and foraged through a bale of singles and tattered paper. At last he produced a grubby business card bearing an official-looking seal and the legend:

Jasper P. Grote
Chief Inspector
NEBRASKA STATE POLICE
POST 229

                                                OMAHA

Valentino's face froze.

The State of Nebraska was the phantom that haunted his recent days. Kalishnikov had said his blackmailer may have been a disgruntled police officer from his hometown, determined to make him pay for an old murder of which he claimed innocence.

"Retired," Grote said. "Five years now. Mandatory, damn their hides. Just an excuse to plug in some sprout in my place and pay him half as much for the same work—which wouldn't be a patch on mine. I cracked some hard nuts in my day, I can tell you." He squinted, bunching his face into a mask of wrinkles. "You okay, son? You're looking a mite peak-ed."

Valentino recovered himself. "I'm just waiting for this conversation to come to a point."

Their waitress chose that moment to bring their meals on a tray: Chicken-fried steak for the tourist, tuna salad for the Californian—with a bowl of tomato soup and the customary crackers sealed in cellophane.

Grote tucked his paper napkin under his collar. "Looky here: Nuked meat and Campbell's canned, just like back home. You'd think this place was part of a chain. The help's cute, though, I'll say that. She dye her hair, you think, or did it come like that out of the flying saucer?" He made that rustling sound in his throat and picked up his fork. "You're curious as to how a pastured-out cop came to be in possession of that there tin."

"I am. Did you seize it in a raid, or—?"

Chewing, the old man shook his head.

"We got lives apart from the force, son. I wasn't born with a badge pinned to my chest. My grandpap was a bike messenger for ten years: Delivered telegrams, groceries, headache pills from the druggist—hell's sake, a jug sometimes, wrapped in brown paper for the old lady that ran the library; anything he could carry in the basket on his handlebars.

"For a spell there in nineteen-twenty, he had steady work pedaling movie reels 'twixt the Roxy The-ay-ter in Broken Bow and the Princess in Berwyn—ten miles it was, give or take. See, in them days the studios out here and back east were tight with their pictures, spread 'em out across two, sometimes three the-ay-ters at a time; on the cheap, see."

Valentino did see. Rolling in money though they were, Fox, MGM, Famous Players-Lasky, and all the rest would force theater owners to share one print with competitors in their area, employing couriers to shuttle the reels back and forth, often miles apart, between showings.

"It was my 'pap's job to collect the first two reels from the Roxy as soon as they were through playing and deliver 'em to the Princess, then when *they* were through, pedal 'em back to the Roxy in time to pick up the *next* two reels and then run 'em over to the Princess, then—well, you get the idea. Twenty miles round trip, twice a day. He died age one hunnert and six, and I'm here to tell you he still had calves big as tractor tires."

He raised his china mug to his lips and sipped. When he made a face, his nose practically met his chin.

"Crankcase oil. *Any*way, this one night, on his second run back to Broken Bow from Berwyn, he clean lost track of the Roxy. It was gone."

"What do you mean gone?"

"Just what I said! Not only the building, but that whole neighborhood: smashed flat by a twister. Not one brick standing on top of another, clear to the courthouse five blocks away and the Woolworth's behind it.

"So there he was, stuck with the first two reels of *Cleopatra* and no place to take 'em. The manager of the Princess had no interest in showing the first two reels of a movie with the rest spread out all over central Nebraska and all his customers dead or scattered just as wide. So 'Pap chucked the cans into his root cellar and there they stayed till the undertaker came to fetch him, and me being his only living relative took possession of all his goods and chattel."

Valentino poked at his tuna salad, doing mental math. There were digits missing. "When did he die?"

Grote chewed, calculated. "Be twenty-two years come December."

"And you've hung on to those two reels all this time?"

"Well, you may not think it, but being chief inspector in the Omaha P.D. don't leave much more time for whittlin' than any of them flat-bellied detectives in Los Angeles." He pronounced it *An-ja-leez*. "It took a gold-plated watch and a testimonial dinner to give me the time to spare; and let me tell you, a man assembles a heap of bric-a-brac in a hunnert and six years. I counted sixteen rocking chairs in his spare room, all broken, and twenny-two cans of Maxwell House coffee in the corncrib. All's *I* had was my grandpap's own word to prove that twister ever happened till a couple of months ago, when the tins turned up amongst the radishes and turnips all gone to sprout in the dugout basement."

"That old nitrate stock needs to be stored in a controlled climate," Valentino said. "It must have been vinegar by the time you found it."

"No such a durn thing. A well-dug root cellar in Custer County stays forty degrees year 'round, come blizzard or bake."

"But afterwards: Twenty-two years—"

Grote swallowed a gravy-soaked morsel of bread and sat back, picking his teeth with a thumbnail. "A man in my work makes lots of friends in lots of places, even some who know more'n a little bit about putting things in special storage. Don't ask me for specifics; I allow as them smocks know what they're doing and I don't. I do know they fixed 'em up in new containers. I hung on to the old tins—to remember my grandpap by, you might say. I brung just this one, figuring it's all you'd need to check my bona fides."

It all made sense; although in today's world anyone was capable of ferreting out enough of the basics of film preservation to support his story.

There was a hole in it nonetheless.

"You said your grandfather had the theater job in nineteen-twenty. That's three years after *Cleopatra* was released."

The old man brought out that baggy grin.

"I forgot you're just a sprout. You're used to a big-ticket picture show coming out all across the country, Sheboygan and Chicago, Denver and Duluth, all on the same day. In 'Pap's time—tarnation, in mine, come to that—they oozed out slow as blackstrap, first on one coast, then t'other, and lastly into what you so-phisticated folk call the Heartland, though we never do, those of us that live there. Hell's sake, Broken Bow and Berwyn didn't see *The Champ* till little Jackie Cooper was practically collecting Social Security."

Valentino knew that, of course. He'd set a trap that his prey was too wily to spring.

He pushed aside his plate—ignored the bowl of soup forming a skin on its surface—and beat a fresh tattoo on the can in his lap. "What are your terms?"

The reaction he got was unexpected. Grote's face suddenly contracted into a mask of discomfort; it was like watching a sheet of paper crumpling in the heat of a flame. He clamped both hands on the edge of the table and hoisted himself to his feet.

"Excuse me, son. I got to go bleed the goose." He scrambled bowlegged down the narrow hall leading to the restrooms.

Just then the front door whooshed open against the air pressure from outside and Leo Kalishnikov came in.

He was dressed entirely out of character: black Lakers ball cap, a hoodie to match, and carpenter's jeans stuffed into the tops of dusty Wellingtons. He blinked in the incandescent glare, cast a broad, uneasy glance about the room, brightened when he spotted Valentino, and scurried his way, propelling himself on what appeared to be a twisted brown Irish shillelagh in one fist.

The development was so bizarre, so entirely unexpected, that several minutes—and some almost incomprehensible conversation—passed before Valentino realized that Jasper Grote (if that was his indeed his name) wasn't coming back from the men's room.

13

KALISHNIKOV DISPENSED WITH his stick—a practiced gesture, exclusive to those accustomed to carrying one—and took the seat Grote had just vacated. The old man's face was ruddier than usual and he was breathing heavily; but his voice retained its astonishing timbre and the rumbling cadence of the steppes of Russia.

"Tell me, my friend; is it only the Philistines who are attracted to the prospect of driving buses, or do the companies actively recruit them? I rang the bell the moment I recognized your automobile outside, and yet we went two long blocks before the barbarous clod condescended to let me off. It seems this quaint establishment is not on the roster of approved stops."

Valentino blinked. Seeing the man so unexpectedly, and in an environment that was so clearly not his natural habitat, had thrown him as thoroughly as Grote's hasty exit.

"You rode a bus all the way from town? I didn't think that was possible."

The other held up a fistful of transfer tickets, fanning them out like a bridge hand. "I had the privilege of putting a transit authority director in touch with a prodigy in the field of electronics, who upgraded his home security system after he was broken into. I borrowed the technology from Fort Knox and the Philadelphia mint. I tell you this in confidence." He reshuffled the tickets and put them away. "I have a drawer filled with these symbols of safe conduct, and tokens enough to take me to Moscow, could buses but float. Logistics are the challenge. The map of all the arteries in the Los Angeles basin resembles the Chinese zodiac."

"Excuse me one moment." Valentino rose, clamping the film can casually against his hip. He went down the narrow hall that Grote had taken, pushed open the door marked MEN, satisfied himself that the room was empty, and went back out. The gridded window in a fire door at the end of the hallway looked out on a patch of gravel, evidently where the employees parked their vehicles. He returned to his table and sat, surreptitiously sliding the film can onto the floor under his chair. Today, for some reason, the long habit of maintaining caution in a competitive profession made him feel like he was keeping a shameful secret. Grote's furtive behavior was contagious.

He spoke quickly, before his tablemate could register the action. "What brought you back this way, apart from buses?"

Kalishnikov's pleated lips spread in a continental smile. At such moments, his tale of a Midwestern upbringing seemed more of a sham than his public pose.

"I was on my way home from an experiment. It occurred to me, now that external speakers are no longer necessary, that the extra space once the mounting poles are removed might accommodate a larger concession stand, able to offer more substantial fare than tradition dictates. If one can order sushi and a garden salad in Dodger Stadium, I fail to see why moviegoers should be forced to content themselves with cotton candy and corn dogs. Perhaps even a comfortable seating area in front of a picture window looking out on the screen, where Papa may nurse a dry martini while Mama minds the menagerie back in the car, or vice versa: I am liberated, you see."

He sighed. "As with any theory, one must visit the actual site to determine if it's practical. I failed to take into account the size and variety of the mosquitoes in this fair valley." He scratched at a ruddy lump on the side of his neck.

"I assume from your enthusiasm that it was worth the exposure."

The old man shifted positions in his chair, grimaced, reached inside a slash pocket, and laid a heavy-duty flashlight in a black rubber case on the table with a clunk.

"A handy bludgeon, when not being employed for illumination," he said. "One never knows when a coyote will make its appearance. *War and Peace* left its impression—wolves, you know, and overturned sleighs." He shrugged. "Practical, yes; if we can persuade Comrade Schwartz to surrender a dozen or so of his parking spaces. Quantity is not quality, if one can couple the price of admission with the quality of the experience."

"So long as we don't lose sight of the fact that drive-ins are a family affair," said Valentino. "Martinis and sushi go with baby-sitters; allowing Mama and Papa to avoid that expense is crucial. In order to get them on board, cotton candy and corn dogs are the answer, without going into competition with Spago's."

"Children, such a bother they are!" Kalishnikov threw up his hands. Then his face changed; his companion saw the connection and guessed where the conversation was headed.

"You have made progress on my difficulty, yes?"

"Maybe. When you came in, did you see the man who was sitting where you are now?"

"Between the sooty skies of the Golden West after twilight and the unconscionably bright electric bulbs of middle-class country dining, I was fortunate to find *you*."

"He saw you; or at least I think he did. Evidently he wanted to avoid a meeting."

"I fervently hope I did not interrupt a romantic liaison. Understand, I make no judgments."

"He wouldn't be my type, even if I were so inclined." That pattern of speech was hard not to pick up. "He says his name is Jasper Grote. Does it mean anything?"

"Apart from an unfortunate arrangement of ugly consonants, nothing at all. A patron of the arts, *n'est-ce pas?* The most generous supporters come frequently from less-than-genteel places, with names to match."

"He says he's from Nebraska."

Did the man flinch? It seemed he did, if only it was the twitch of one heavy eyelid. Valentino was watching closely, and may have assigned too much importance to it.

In any case the response was bland.

"One meets them on occasion. The Lord knows there is not much in the Cornhusker State to hold them there. Even the scarecrows stand by the road with their thumbs out."

"Still, the coincidence is tough to ignore." He described the man.

The other looked thoughtful, then shook his head.

"Could he be my blackmailer?"

"I don't know. He came to me with something that might be just a pretext, to get close and find out what I know. I'm on my way back to my office to see what I can find out. If he's our man, I can play along with his story; keep him on the hook long enough to gather evidence against him. That should frighten him off."

From another pocket Kalishnikov unshipped a watch on the end of a gold chain long enough to strangle a man and popped open the lid. "You keep long hours, my friend."

With a start, Valentino realized how dark it was outside. Harriet must think he'd been shanghaied by pirates. He hauled out his phone. SERVICE UNAVAILABLE. He put it back and signaled for his check. "Tomorrow morning. Can I offer you a ride?"

"I was hoping you would. The last bus has run." Kalishnikov traded the timepiece for his shillelagh and stretched his free hand across the table, laying it upon Valentino's. "Pray do not give up on my daughter. I should like to see her, even if she has become as much of a scoundrel as her sire."

The archivist disengaged himself from the hand. "All I can do is promise to try." He stooped to recover the film can, feeling as he did so like some kind of Judas. Grote's story meant more to him than just a stall to catch a crook. Had he come to this, placing a few hundred feet of celluloid ahead of an old man's fears and dreams? If so, what was there to separate him from his closest competitor? When it came to the chase, Teddie Goodman was never far from his thoughts.

In the parking lot, light from one of the tall poles fell on a scrap of paper clamped under his windshield wiper. As Kalishnikov was climbing in on the passenger's side, Valentino snatched it free. Jasper Grote's business card was folded around a purple tab with ADMIT ONE printed on it in silver. On the back of the card, someone had scribbled in uneven block letters:

MIDNIGHT TO-MORROW

14

WITH SOME DIFFICULTY—AND fresh shame, for the man was clearly lonely—Valentino declined Kalishnikov's invitation to come in for a hundred-proof nightcap, but promised to report on the progress of the investigation.

On the way back across town, he blessed the late-night yellow flashers that waved him through intersections without stopping. His phone service was back, but he doubted an apology call at this point would mollify Harriet.

But the thought made him smile. It was good to have someone to worry about him.

Century City is nearly as self-contained as its name implies; it thrives with little input from the metropolis that surrounds it. The community occupies the old Fox lot, where the movies began. On that site, William Fox had rolled the dice throughout the first quarter of the twentieth century, betting every penny of profit on studio construction, technical innovation, and a nationwide chain of theaters until he crapped out spectacularly, a victim of his own ambition and the Crash of 1929. Somewhere in this glittering complex of hotels, malls, restaurants, hospitals, and high-rise apartment buildings, Theda Bara—Fox's own discovery—had woven her primitive spell: But just where, under all that steel and concrete, was as much a mystery as the woman herself.

How odd, Valentino thought, that after a century she should find her way back home.

The hour was late for the working residents of Harriet's building, and most of the windows were dark. Hers, however, blazed down at him accusingly as he climbed the front steps. He pushed her call button and waited an anxious moment before the buzzer let him into the foyer and upstairs to her condominium.

He found her sitting at her work table in front of the windows, peering into the twin eyepieces of her microscope. She wore a smock that covered her to the knees, below which showed her green silk pajamas and slippered feet.

"I'm sorry I didn't—"

She shushed him. "Comparing skin cells. We're talking about a man's life. If what you have to say is more important than that, go ahead and interrupt."

He grinned; he didn't buy it. She was only pretending to be preoccupied with science stuff. It played better than the role of the neglected girlfriend. She abhorred clichés as much as he, old-movie fanatic that he was, embraced them.

He approached the table, apparently without her notice. Holding his breath, he slid Jasper Grote's business card under one of the lenses and the admissions ticket under the other.

She jumped. "What the hell do you think you're—"

But she was too much the scientist not to seek the answer for herself. Leaning in, she twisted the adjustment knobs this way and that, closing first one eye, then the other, until he was sure she was drawing out the drama just to punish him. When at last she stopped to study the images, he waited a beat, then turned the business card over so she could read the words on the other side.

After a moment she sat back, looking at him with one of those expressions he couldn't read; she had a whole vocabulary.

"So are you and Jasper P. Grote going steady, or is this just a one-night stand?"

For answer he held up the film can, which he'd been hiding behind his hip.

She read the stenciled label at a glance. Years of staring at minute particles through powerful lenses hadn't spoiled her eyesight; in fact they seemed to have made it sharper.

"Oh, *her!*" She looked up. "Hath age not withered her, nor custom staled her infinite variety?"

"Shrapnel and Shakespeare; how did you manage to study both?" No reaction. He stopped grinning. "Anyway, you met Grote here in this room. Your description was spot-on, by the way."

"I didn't get this job by answering an ad on the subway. So Grote's his name. You found him."

"He found me." He told her about the meeting at The Comet.

Her expression changed. "Val, that's disturbing. This is Hollywood. The department has a whole division devoted to stalking crimes. It's not the cavalry. It rarely shows up in the nick of time; practically never."

"He seems harmless enough." *To me, anyway.* He left that unsaid.

She watched him retrieve the two items from the microscope. "And this harmless character has arranged a midnight meeting in some undisclosed location to prove just how harmless he is. Does he expect you to find the place in a city that has more movie houses than parking garages? If it *is* a movie house," she added. "I can get a ticket just like that at Chuck E. Cheese."

"Admission tickets that come on rolls are always red or yellow or blue, sometimes green. Only one place in Southern California prints them in silver on purple. It sells the best caramel corn in Southern California."

"And of course a fellow connoisseur can't possibly be the Zodiac Killer."

He shook the film can. "This isn't exactly candy from a stranger. It's a lot of trouble to go to just to snare one minor academic."

"I detect the distinct lack of rattle. How do you know it ever held what it says?"

"Well, that's where you come in."

"YOU'RE ASKING FOR one of the most sophisticated scientific teams in the world to examine a hundred-year-old film can to find out if it's authentic? What's the matter with the UCLA lab?"

They were sitting now on opposite ends of her twelve-foot couch, the biggest piece of furniture on the premises; a thing of no aesthetic value and about as comfortable as the seating in a fast-food restaurant. She seemed to have purchased it specifically for its length, which invited plenty of neutral space when intimacy wasn't desired.

"Hear me out before you *throw* me out," he said. "This one's hush-hush. The Film Preservation Department is a gossip factory. If the administration fired every underpaid technician and janitor for selling tips to the competition, I'd be washing beakers and emptying wastebaskets myself." He rattled his nails against the flat tin. "It's Theda Bara, remember. Teddie Goodman thinks she has exclusive rights to her entire body of work; she even nicked Bara's unpublished memoirs from the University of Cincinnati just to have them in her house. Instead of thanking Turkus for buying her out of a felony conviction, she told him he should have spent a little more and given her the memoirs as a present in return for her loyal service."

"He should've fired her."

"She's the Turk's most valuable asset. Teddie puts the 'super' in Supernova International. And she won't rest until the world agrees she has a blood tie to the Vamp of Vamps."

"She doesn't, you said."

"At this point she's told so many people she's a great-great-grandniece or a cousin five times removed or somebody's lovechild, she may actually believe she was *born* Theodosia Goodman, just like Theda; as if she didn't just take the name. You've seen yourself how quickly the fangs and claws come out when she gets a whiff of cinema gold; do you think she'd stop short of stealing *Cleopatra* and claim it as her birthright?"

"I don't want to think about her at all. But what could Grote want to see you about? He already gave you the can. The next move should be yours."

Valentino hesitated. If he shared with her his suspicions about Grote's true motives, she'd insist he back out of the deal; and if the man was Kalishnikov's blackmailer, she'd be right. But during the drive home he'd convinced himself he was being paranoid.

The name the old man had used, and his description, had meant nothing to Kalishnikov. Grote might have sensed the "Russian" was there to see Valentino, and didn't want to discuss his proposition in a stranger's presence. The fact that he'd come with the ticket suggested he'd already decided on a second meeting.

"These rural types are born horse traders," Valentino said. "Maybe he wants to discuss his terms in detail before we shake hands on the deal."

Harriet crossed her legs and waggled a bare foot. She'd parked the smock at her work station and poured herself a glass of Chablis. It was almost one A.M., long past the deadline she set herself for drinking during the workweek. She hadn't poured one for Valentino.

"Here you had me thinking you'd stayed out with the lawn furniture because you were busy doing your job, when all the time you were working up the courage to ask me to risk mine."

"And here *I* thought you were mad at me because I didn't call to tell you I'd be late. I *am* sorry about dinner."

"Apology accepted, as to dinner. As to the other, rubbish. You're a guest in my home. Where you go and how long you stay out isn't my business until you decide it is. Same here. You're not Lucy and I'm not Ricky."

"Shouldn't that be the other way around?"

"I can't promise anything," she said. "A metal can is inorganic. It can't be carbon-dated to determine age."

"That much I know. It's the ink that concerns me. In those days before synthetics, printers' ink—the kind used to stencil the production's title and date on the lid—was composed of pigment and varnish. The varnish was prepared from linseed oil, rosin, and soap, all organic compounds. If it's chemical, it's phony; simple as that.

"Try to scrape off just enough of a sample to run a test," he added. "If the film never shows, but the can turns out to be genuine, the original container is worth something to museums and private collectors. Turkus himself might bid on it at auction. That would add a chunk to the department's budget."

"I hope it's enough for one more hire, because if my supervisor gets wind of it I'll be out of a job."

"So you'll do it?"

She bounced her foot twice more, then got up and went into the kitchenette, where she filled another glass and brought it out to him.

15

"YOU LOOK LIKE an extra in a George Romero film," Kyle Broadhead said. "Tinseltown nightlife track you down at last?"

It was one of those rare precious days when the wind from the Pacific blew strong enough to boot the smog clear over the San Bernardino Mountains, painting L.A. in the soft pastels of a vintage picture postcard. Unhappily for Valentino, he hadn't been able to appreciate it. He peeled the sunglasses away from his bloodshot eyes and leaned for support against the copying machine the professor was using. Yesterday had run long, and he was no night owl.

"You might say I caught the double feature at the Comet. You should need a passport to visit the Valley."

"Wail your blues to somebody who didn't warn you." Broadhead went on feeding sheets into the machine from a shallow stack. The motor hummed, stuttered, and delivered the copies onto the tray with a sort of hen's cackle at the end of each printing.

Valentino pointed at the text on the topmost page. It appeared to be an exhaustive exposition of one line in the 1933 motion-picture adaptation of *Alice in Wonderland*; a line that didn't appear in Lewis Carroll. The word "psycho-symmetrical" leapt out at him. It wasn't every day a layman contributed something new to the lexicon of the mental-health specialist.

"You read me that passage a year ago. How many drafts does this make? I'm starting to think you write all day, then spend all night throwing away what you wrote, like Penelope unraveling her knitting."

"Homer, the lad throws at me." The other shook his head. "I told you when you were a sniveling sophomore not to waste your time on trash. Correct me in my advanced state of dementia, but were you not the one who nagged me to get up off my fat academe and *write* the book?"

"It never occurred to me it'd take you as long as *Gone with the Wind.*"

"Nor did the size of the undertaking. In the old days, each studio in the Dream Factory cranked out a new film every week; that's five, not counting Poverty Row. Now, with Netflix, Hulu, A&E, Showtime, and God knows how many others stirred into the mix, just keeping up with the new releases is like drinking soup in a downpour. *The Persistence of Vision* got me tenure; but that was when you could count the major studios on the fingers of one hand, and they were too busy competing with *The Beverly Hillbillies* to give me a paragraph of decent copy. *Beach Blanket Bingo?* Deliver me from evil! I was young, lean, and hungry then. If I were just one of those things now, I might be able to dictate a semi-respectable first draft from my deathbed."

The room—designed originally as a utility closet, back when the building supplied power to the university campus—was just big enough to contain the monster copier, shelves of office supplies, and two members of the film preservation team; if one of them stood sideways. Valentino checked the time on his phone. "Shouldn't you be in class?"

"I put in an appearance yesterday. My teaching assistant's full of promptitude and vinegar. He can take charge of the Mongol horde till Friday, when I hand out the weekend assignments. I wouldn't trade the pleasure of seeing those crestfallen faces for a sabbatical in the Bahamas."

"You've been threatening it for years: Ten thousand words on *Ivan the Terrible*, parts one and two."

"And three."

"He never filmed part three."

"And the first student who brings that to my attention gets to be my next T.A."

"Speaking of impossible quests," said Valentino.

Minutes into the narrative, Broadhead stopped threading paper into the machine and turned it off. Even omitting Valentino's suspicions of Jasper Grote's motives and Kalishnikov's personal ordeal, it was worthy of the professor's close attention.

He frowned into the middle ground. "It's plausible, on the face of it. I had the same job in my callow youth, shuttling reels back and forth between picture houses on my old Schwinn. The hours were long and the pay just about kept me in new tires, but I caught the bug, and you can see where it led."

Valentino almost missed what Broadhead said next; he was trying to picture him straddling a bicycle.

The other shook his head. "Doesn't figure. Nothing so trivial as a killer tornado would keep the studios from recovering those lost reels. They look after their product like blood diamonds."

"Maybe they weren't so conscientious a hundred years ago," Valentino said. "Those were the days before re-releases and home video. Audiences demanded something new all the time, and there wasn't room to store new footage *and* old, with no market for the old. Maybe they just declared the reels a dead loss, looking to make up for them on the next Chaplin."

"'Maybe' doesn't get you into Theda Bara's pants, my boy. It isn't like you not to come charging in here with the evidence, slavering like a pit bull."

"I left the can with Harriet to run the tests. She's pushing it up the priority list right now, if her supervisor isn't looking."

"Cops involved already. That's a record for you."

"I thought it best not to dawdle. If Teddie Goodman gets wind this one's in play, yesterday is too late. What we need to do—"

"What do you mean 'we,' paleface? I turned in my Captain Midnight decoder ring last time. Spies, spooks, and slinky dames aren't on the syllabus this semester. From now on I'll take my chances with paper cuts and chalk dust."

"Grease pencils, now. You *have* been out of the classroom a long time." Valentino's grin faded. "So you're not the slightest bit interested in whether Cleopatra climbs back out of her tomb somewhere in the Sahara."

"Don't be a dunce. I'm not ready for interment myself. I'm confident, based on our long association and the wisdom it's been my privilege to share, that Fanta and I will be at the Oracle opening night, compliments of the management. Between her legal training and my vast knowledge of the medium, we'll provide the missing reels from our imagination. After all, any freshman with a cursory knowledge of ancient history knows how the story ends."

"They say it wasn't really an asp. That's a myth."

"Keep it under your hat. Bitch-goddesses don't die of the sniffles."

Valentino sighed dramatically. "Just as well you can't tag along tonight; I have only one of these." He held up the purple ticket. Broadhead squinted at it.

"Glad to see the dump hasn't been torn down. I was feeling sorry for the rats."

His protégé produced a six-page tabloid from a hip pocket

and unfolded it to the advertising section. "It's still standing, according to *El Anuncio*. I picked up this copy in a coffee house in Westwood Village. It's showing all this week."

Eyes framed in black kohl glared out from a quarter-page advertisement, pursed red lips below. Across the stylized illustration ran a quote in boldface: "Kiss me, my fool!"

"I'm not sure which astounds me more," Broadhead said, "that a creaky period piece like *A Fool There Was* can draw enough of an audience to run a week, or that you spent part of your university salary on an underground newspaper."

"It was free. I went to three places looking for it. My Nebraska peace officer left the ticket on my windshield, with an invitation to drop in tonight at midnight."

"And of course you wanted to find out what was playing, in case the meeting turned out a disappointment. How did your mystery man arrange a screening of Bara's first picture on such short notice?"

"Maybe it was coincidence. More likely he did some shopping around before he approached me, counting on a dead movie queen to help close the sale. You've said it yourself, Kyle: The City of Angels is haunted by its past. At least one of its hundreds of revival theaters is bound to be showing what you want on any given night." He rolled a shoulder. "Sure, I was curious about the feature. If the deal turned out to be a bust, I'd at least get a night's free entertainment. Also it's been a year since I visited the place. I wanted to make sure it was still there in case I was being lured into a trap."

"Why a trap, apart from the dubious hour? Have you fallen into trouble already? Another record bites the dust!"

Valentino faltered; he hadn't meant to tip his hand. He forced a grin onto his exhausted face.

"Intrigued? I bet there are some seats left. It's not exactly *Spider-Man Versus the Incredible Hulk.*"

He was still holding up the ticket. The professor stared at it, unconsciously drumming his fingers on his pile of manuscript. Plainly he was tempted. Finally he shook himself, like an old dog caught in the rain.

"It's your show. I'm fairly certain the invitation didn't come with a plus-one. Just let me know how the picture comes out; not well, if memory serves, for the leading man. Also as I recall, there's no concession stand in the lobby. A man of my reputation can't be seen smuggling Milk Duds into an all-night grindhouse. Anticlimactic, this rendezvous, is it not? Grote seems to have concluded your first encounter satisfactorily."

Valentino dismissed that with another shrug, lest he talk himself back into his earlier fears. He was glad Broadhead hadn't called his bluff. An uninvited third party could botch the deal.

At the same time he was disappointed. Domesticity so late in his life had robbed his mentor of his lust for adventure. Valentino wondered if his own devotion to Harriet would affect him the same way someday.

He turned and grasped the doorknob.

"Did I dismiss you?"

The tempered steel in Kyle's tone stopped him cold. He hadn't heard it since graduation. He turned back. The professor had picked up his copied pages and was drumming them into order on top of the machine.

"Before you wander into the woods like Hansel and Gretel on the promise of nothing but a rusty can full of air, don't you think you should check Grote's story?"

"How—?"

"Next time you visit your favorite section in the library, try pulling your nose out of the Coming Attractions columns and look at the headlines. How do you even know there *was* a tornado in Broken Bow, Nebraska, in nineteen-twenty? Or if there was a Roxy to begin with?"

He tucked his book, the original along with the copy, under one arm. "You're out of practice. I see now that my day, which included brunch with the dean, counseling a grad student, and shaking my cup at an alumni fundraiser, is not over. It seems I'm to pay a visit downtown and fill in the blanks you overlooked."

"The library closes at nine."

"So it does—to everyone who didn't tutor the security chief's son in Entertainment Law. The idiot scored a passing grade." He fished an electronic key card from a vest pocket and brandished it like a handgun. "Enjoy the show, you night-blooming jasmine. Don't spoil it by thinking about me shut up in a dusty room—a man with my allergies—doing your homework for you, like the fat little boy for his neighborhood bully."

"Thanks, Kyle. Don't know what I'd do without you."

"Me neither. But I'm inured to my many faults."

Valentino left, suppressing the urge to whistle. His fish was hooked.

16

MIDNIGHT WAS AGES away. The only way to accelerate the progress of time was to keep busy. Once again Valentino made the rounds of his sources, but Leo Kalishnikov's daughter remained as elusive as at the beginning.

Back in his office, Valentino processed some papers that had been breeding dust mites for months, discarding correspondence long past its expiration date, filing possible leads to missing-but-not-quite-lost films and TV episodes in the folder marked PENDING, and entering contact numbers in the computer for the purpose of acquiring features to show at The Oracle; for instance, he lacked only *Baby Face Nelson* to fill out his plans for a week-long retrospective commemorating Mickey Rooney's centennial (delayed two years by the pandemic): "From Andy Hardy to America's Most Wanted: The Long Life of a Short Subject." It was an off-beat idea; just the vehicle, he hoped, to draw attention to the theater's recovery from the latest round of construction. The noise from upstairs had forced him to suspend matinee showings until his private bathroom was completed.

He grew drowsy by mid-afternoon. Factoring in yesterday's extended hours, excitement over the chance to acquire *Cleopatra*, his stymied efforts to get to the bottom of Leo Kalishnikov's dilemma—which if they failed might cause the theater designer to withdraw his partnership in the Comet enterprise and oblige Valentino himself to invest in an old friend's quixotic fancy— he'd had fewer than four hours' sleep in twenty-four. At this rate he'd never make it to a midnight meeting with Grote. He shut everything down and went out to tell Ruth he was going home. For once the old Gorgon was too busy applying a fresh coat of fire-engine-red to her nails to pass judgment on his work ethic.

Part of his problem with sleeping at Harriet's, he knew, was that he didn't feel at home there. They'd made no pledge toward permanent housekeeping arrangements. Her place was emphatically her own, with only a small array of his own clothing and toiletries to suit his convenience. Weeks past deadline, The Oracle's latest round of improvements promised only more din, additional dust, and unpredictable interruptions in plumbing and electricity; but the place belonged to him in a way Harriet's never would, regardless of his feelings for her: It was home.

A shroud of opaque plastic, erected to contain debris, barred him from his cot in the projection booth. He took refuge in the auditorium, whose soundproof walls kept the whine of electric drills and roar of reciprocating saws at bay. The row of plush-upholstered reclining chairs Kalishnikov had insisted on installing at the rear of the orchestra ("My friend, your wealthier customers will pay triple the standard rate to reserve such splendid accommodations!") promised all the luxury of a queen-sized bed. With pandemonium going on upstairs, past the coffered ceiling with its gilt cherubs in relief, the place was as silent as a Buddhist temple. He dreamed that he and Errol Flynn were close friends, and awoke wondering if collecting stamps wouldn't be a healthier use of his free time.

He didn't know where he was at first. Little light filtered in from outside, leaving most of the illumination to the pale blue glow of the diamond-shaped LEDs installed in the aisle risers to direct customers to their seats. He fished out his phone: 6:17. Almost six hours to go.

Outside the auditorium the building was silent; or as close to it as a nearly century-old construction ever came. The ocean-borne wind continued unabated; the timber framework, hewn from pre-Dutch disease elms, groaned and sighed with each gust.

The work crew had decamped to some mysterious competing project, taking all but the least portable equipment with them. He went upstairs, peeled aside the plastic sheeting, and looked for signs of progress, but could make nothing of the tarpaulin-draped interior beyond a war-torn ruin of broken plaster and tentacles of frayed wiring protruding from gaping holes in the walls. The Spartan flat he shared with the massive twin Bell & Howell projectors (a requirement of the vintage three-D pro-cess) looked as far from reach as ever they had during the years of renovation. He wondered if the loss of revenue while the work was going on was worth the conveniences of sink, shower, and commode to the resident, and if his audience would come back once it was finished. The anxiety was nothing new: As Broadhead had put it, The Oracle was "Custer's Last Stand, playing on a continuous loop."

On the way down the sweeping grand staircase, he felt suddenly light-headed and grasped the brass handrail for sup-port. He hadn't eaten since tuna salad and Campbell's soup in the country restaurant twenty hours ago. He locked up and drove to The Brass Gimbal.

The restaurant catered to industry insiders, and was where Valentino and his colleagues hung out to talk shop.

The building, once a residential hotel for unmarried women,

was nondescript apart from its entrance. The present owners had salvaged the twin copper-framed doors from The Peacock, a demolished motion-picture palace in Pasadena; but it was still the dinner hour in laid-back L.A., and the crowd gathered in front obscured the eponymous bird etched across both leaded-glass panes from view.

He didn't get out of the car. Broadhead and Harriet could be trusted to keep their mouths shut about what he was up to; not so much the rest of his friends, who might wheedle it out of him. Hollywood was a small town for all its sprawl, and the competition in his field was savage. He drove on.

Suddenly every eatery he passed was a fishbowl, potentially aswim with fine finned friends. His stomach rumbled and his head ached, but he continued his quest.

Then, cresting a hill, he spotted the obscene pink of a gigantic synthetic wiener nestled in a garish yellow bun, straddling a square hut with a serving window in front. Here, too, there was a crowd, but many of the loiterers were pointing cameras at companions poised grinning in front of the cheesy landmark: Tourists. Film Factory professionals avoided them like a virus.

He joined the line waiting to order, taking cover behind sunglasses and turning away from the street whenever a car cruised past, like a fugitive in a *noir* picture. In front of him was a sixtyish couple in loud shirts and fanny packs, who when they got to the window squinted at the menu board and argued over sodium levels. Between the maddening smell of hot grease and their interminable bickering, he felt faint.

"Professor!"

The voice (Jersey Shore, if he had to guess) repeated the greeting twice before he turned to respond. A squat figure sat on the bulbous front bumper of a gargantuan black auto parked against the curb, shoveling cheese fries from a cardboard basket into his mouth. His wardrobe had been assembled from an upholstery warehouse, and a thatch of improbably black hair perched on his head like a divot.

Professor; he should have known. No one else in the archivist's orbit mistook him for a member of faculty.

Henry Anklemire. Director of Information Services in the department that employed Valentino: formerly the aluminum siding king of Brooklyn, New York; Time Share Hank in Costa Rica; the man to see for gently used furniture in Phoenix; and positively the last of all his fellow workers he wanted to see at that moment. But the little man was indispensable to the department's budget, and not to be slighted. Valentino surrendered his place in line and went over.

"Didn't know you Ivy League types slummed around this neighborhood. Dog?" Anklemire rattled a greasy paper sack.

The other started to decline, but his digestive juices drowned him out. "I don't want to mooch off your lunch."

"I'd just throw it away. I forget I'm not a teenager no more, scarfing up my weight in blintzes and bagels. It's a sin to waste food." He shook the bag.

Valentino withdrew a hot dog wrapped in a brown paper napkin and sat down next to him. The car's bumper was as solid as a girder, and bore bulgy growths like chrome-plated tree galls. "How'd you come by the aircraft carrier?"

"Like it? It's a Roadmaster: A classic. I got it in a police auction in Miami; I was down there speculating in real estate at the time. Dope dealer shipped it in from Havana with half a million in coke stashed in the muffler. Mighta got away with it, too, if a Dade County sheriff didn't pull him over for excessive noise two miles from the beach."

The hot dog was smothered with onions, relish, and a variety of mustard that blistered his tongue. It made him gasp. Seeing his distress, Anklemire reached into the sack and brought out a

Sprite in a cup the size of a silo. Ice shifted noisily inside. "No cooties, honest! Didn't touch it."

He watched his companion put out the fire. "What's the skinny, Maestro? Onto anything that might put some kopecks in the old company mattress?"

Valentino was surprised to find himself wanting to confide in the shameless hustler. Maybe running into him wasn't such bad luck after all. Of all those who'd taken up residence there, Anklemire alone seemed to be immune to the Hollywood mystique, or at least blind to its romance. He would carry no tales. Valentino took another draw from the straw.

"Theda Bara. I don't suppose you've ever heard of her."

The little man beamed all over.

"Aunt Theo! I ain't thought of her in years."

17

AUNT THEO. **NOTHING** recently (apart from the possible acquisition of *Cleopatra*) had struck the archivist with such force as
those two words. There were hardcore silent-film buffs who
didn't know Bara's real name was Theodosia Goodman.

"You *knew* her?"

Henry Anklemire lifted one corner of his lip, exposing some
of the teeth he'd had made to his order in Tijuana.

"Professor, I can read your mind like the weekend receipts.
'Just how old *is* this schmoe?' you're thinking. Not so old as
that. She was years out of showbiz then. I only knew about the
other name from something my old man let drop. She was my
babysitter."

"Back East?" Doubt crept in. He knew Bara had lived in Los
Angeles from early in her career to her death in 1955. Anklemire
was practically a poster child for Hoboken.

"Hell, no! Not more'n twelve blocks from this spot. She was
our next-door neighbor after the old man got transferred to
Long Beach. I was a navy brat, didn't I ever mention?"

Valentino shook his head. For all he'd known of the little

sharpie's origins, he might have been won in a poker game in Atlantic City.

A confidence for a confidence. Any morsel from cinema history contributed to the value of the memory vault; and anyway, given even a whisper of encouragement, the little PR whiz could sell sausage links in Tel Aviv.

"I may have a chance to acquire *Cleopatra* for the university. The first two reels, anyway."

"*Cleopatra*, yeah." He nodded animatedly. "She had a poster in her living room. I spent as much time there as she did in my folks' place. I can see it now. She had on a brassiere made of gold snakes and another snake around her head, and she was staring holes right through you. Somebody'd scribbled all over it. Damn shame."

"It was *signed*?" The half-eaten hot dog slid off his lap. He'd forgotten it, along with his hunger.

"Could be, come to think. Wasn't all the same handwriting. Some of it was straight Palmer Method, others I coulda done better with fingerprint."

An original poster of Theda Bara's most famous picture— possibly the only one in existence—inscribed, evidently, by the cast.

"Do you remember any of it? Names?"

"I was maybe four years old, Professor. I could barely read. You got a point, though. It must've meant something to spend good money getting it framed." He helped himself to a scoop of chili and chewed thoughtfully. Then he shook himself. "Anyway, we had to let the house go after the navy give the old man the boot—some misunderstanding over phony government scrip, I think—and we moved to Barstow, where we raised turkeys till somebody complained they was fattened up on gravel. You can't please everybody. I never saw Aunt Theo again, and I heard she died."

Contentedly, as Valentino recalled; living on her canny investments and noodling around with her memoirs, although publishers weren't interested in the autobiography of a forgotten movie star. A decade would pass before a surge in nostalgia rekindled interest in American iconography.

"What do you remember about her?"

"She had a white face—spooky white. Like chalk. Eyes big as ashtrays. Sometimes she'd parade around the room wearing this brown shawl, waving her arms and jabbering—she had a deep voice, deep as a man's. I don't guess none of her fans ever got to hear it. Other times—I dunno, she was a *Bubele*."

"A what?"

"A nana; somebody's grandmother. She had this big jar of hard candy, and she'd pry the lid off and shove it under your nose. Only it was a hundred years old and the pieces was all stuck together. First time I got one loose and chomped on it, I cracked a tooth. After that I'd put it in my mouth, then take it out and stick it in a pocket when she wasn't looking. See, I didn't want to hurt her feelings. She was a nice lady, and I didn't see nothing bad in that *meshugas* with the scarf. Next to my real *Bubele*, Esther the Yenta, she was a shrinkin' violet."

It was Valentino's turn to be silent. Then he turned to face his companion. "I don't suppose you know what became of that poster."

LIKE AREA 51, Genghis Khan's tomb, and the Lost Dutchman mine, the location appeared on no map; its address was known only to its habitual patrons and such skin-of-their-teeth publications as Valentino had managed to disinter from the Bohemian coffee shop (in which, if one was patient, he might score a cup of legitimate coffee); where only the number appeared, sans name or even the identity of the street. The message seemed to be that if you didn't know it, you weren't welcome.

Valentino knew it. It occupied a wedge-shaped lot off South Broadway, a brief stroll from the classic movie houses left over from the Golden Age, which now barely subsisted on a fare of Spanish-language motion pictures aimed at the majority population of East L.A. In this case, the proprietors had only to change the title cards in order to accommodate any native tongue.

Strictly speaking, the place didn't stand so much as exist, as it was invisible above ground level. In the great days of search-lights, live radio coverage, and glamorous patrons who arrived by limousine in full evening dress, The King Henry Theater had used the space to store stage properties and live-show costumes four yards beneath the feet of the patrons. A wrecking ball had taken the original structure around the time of Watergate and a multi-level mall was built on the foundation, housing a video arcade, souvenir shops, and the kind of Mexican restaurants that attracted tourists but were shunned by the local Hispanic population in favor of more authentic establishments a few blocks away. In the meantime a local film society had taken lease on the basement to screen other-than-mainstream features directed at diehard cineastes. Most nights it took in just enough to cover the utilities. It was known—where it was known—entirely unofficially, and coined not by a single person but by a kind of mass telepathy, as The Priest's Hole.

An alley door opened onto a steep flight of steps leading down into dank darkness, smelling vaguely of earth and freshly dug potatoes. In the heat of summer an industrial-size electric fan placed at the base of the stairs stirred the air, which on humid days was thick enough to wrinkle; but on this night in an early Southern California spring it was switched off, allowing the musical accompaniment of whatever was playing onscreen to reach the ears, as well as set the crumbling masonry abuzz, long before Valentino reached the bottom.

There, Theda Bara awaited him in the person of that same abstract image he'd seen in the newspaper: black-framed eyes and scarlet lips on a sandwich-board sign set up on the floor. It served in place of a marquee.

Behind a podium, an emaciated young woman in a snug floor-length black gown waited to take his ticket. Her face was pale almost to the point of transparency and her skeletal hands were cloaked in black fingerless gloves; the fingers that brushed his hand when the exchange was made were as cold as the surrounding stonework.

"Hello, Gladys. How are you? Kids okay?"

The thin face brightened. "Val! Great! Tony made the soccer team and Phyllis is taking tap lessons."

"What happened to the violin?"

"She swapped it for a Pokémon card collection."

He slid a five-dollar bill into the pickle jar propped on the podium and parted a curtain, entering the auditorium (for lack of a more appropriate name). No popcorn machine or candy display distracted him from this route; the operating budget couldn't support health department requirements. Customers were sternly discouraged from smuggling in treats from outside, lest paper sacks, Styrofoam containers, and plastic straws attract the attention of the fire marshal.

The auditorium was a rectangular space, narrow but deep. Mismatched tables supported lamps in the corners, their fifteen-watt bulbs glowing through red Gypsy scarves draped over the shades; these, along with the funnel-shaped light spilling from the projector at the rear of the room, provided just enough illumination to guide him to his seat. Rows of folding metal chairs faced a muslin screen stretched over three sheets of four-by-eight plywood.

Valentino, who might have been expected to sneer at the bare-bones set-up, reveled in it. It was just such a place where movies were born, in candy stores and barbershops long enough to project flickering features when Taft was president, without refreshment (and certainly without a soundtrack) for the benefit of audiences curious about this latest innovation at the dawn of the American Century. An elderly woman, as stout as Gladys was thin, sat at an electric keyboard (the most modern thing in the room) on a raised platform to the left of the screen, banging away at "Flight of the Bumblebee" while Harry Houdini, suspended upside-down from a crane multiple stories above a city street, wriggled his way out of a straitjacket. Apart from the live music, the film clicking through the gate of the projector was the only sound.

The newsreel finished and the screen went blank while the projectionist changed reels. Someone coughed; a solitary sound among the dozen or so visitors scattered about the room. No sign of Jasper Grote. Valentino hoped his and Jasper Grote's tickets had helped the midnight program show a profit; the convenience of streaming, Turner Classic Movies, and affordable DVDs had bitten into the once-thriving local market in films not to be found at the neighborhood Cineplex. Audiences not familiar with the experience of watching a movie in the company of strangers, reacting to each thrill in concert with others (at that moment, they were strangers no longer), would never know what they missed.

The lady at the piano took advantage of the interruption to flex her fingers and sip something yellow from a glass tumbler; then as the clicking resumed she rearranged her music sheets, adjusted her bifocals, and teased a series of anticipatory chords from the ivories. The archivist felt that old familiar rise in his heart rate as the digits appeared on the screen, counting down from ten; then there sprang before him, in white letters on black, a succession of title cards:

"A FOOL THERE WAS"
A WILLIAM FOX PRODUCTION
Starring
EDWARD JOSÉ
Directed by
                                        FRANK POWELL

Theda Bara's name did not appear until the next card, among the supporting players; such was the story of so many screen immortals, from Rudolph Valentino to Greta Garbo, Clark Gable to Lana Turner, Joan Crawford to John Wayne, Julia Roberts to Kevin Costner.

But instead of the first scene, another notice, printed in plain black on white, appeared next:

RESTORATION
BY
SYLVIA TURKUS LABS
A DIVISION OF
                                    SUPERNOVA INTERNATIONAL LLC

His reaction to this was mixed. As a cinema maven, he applauded this triumph over the ravages of time and public indifference to the fate of historical relics, while his professional side chafed at his loss to a competitor. UCLA had bid on the film's restoration rights, but Mark David Turkus (ostensibly in memory of his late mother, Sylvia) had a bigger bank balance.

Something rustled at his side; a latecomer settling into the adjacent seat; another annoyance yet, that someone would invade his space with so many other vacancies to choose from. Then came a voice to his ear:

"You snooze, you lose. I don't guess it would make you feel any better if I told you that that was as high as I was permitted to bid. Think of it: One dollar more and it would be UCLA up there on the screen."

Valentino started. He recognized the throaty contralto even when its owner spoke in a whisper. He knew before turning his head that the interloper was Teddie Goodman.

18

VALENTINO COULD NEVER decide if his chief rival in the film restoration business was beautiful; whether the effect she had on everyone she met was natural or cosmetic or simply a matter of personality. Certainly she packaged herself to make a striking impression, sheathing her slender form in skintight outfits in arresting shades, exotically patterned and cut at eccentric angles, shaping and polishing her nails to alien perfection, applying makeup with a scalpel, and either pinning her blue-black hair up as high as a bishop's miter or letting it fall to her (usually bare) shoulders like a spill of melted licorice. The intention, of course, was to bolster her claim to a blood relationship with the Vamp of Vamps, but in practice she was more Theda than Theda herself; faithful to the fancy rather than the fact. As Kyle Broadhead had put it, if Theda Bara were to enter a Theda Bara look-alike contest, she would place second behind Teddie Goodman.

Today she wore something that shimmered when she moved, but whose details were vague in the ghostly dark. Valentino, recovering from shock, opened his mouth to ask why she was there, or how she'd found him, or if she had to be back in her box of native earth before sunrise; but before he could utter a word, a scimitar-shaped fingernail touched red lips and a jet-trail eyebrow twitched in the direction of the screen, where the most *fatale* of *femmes* was preparing to draw first blood.

Although conversation couldn't detract from a feature played out in title cards rather than spoken dialogue, he clapped his mouth shut and settled back into his seat. Explanations could wait: He refused to let this ghost at the banquet interfere with enjoying the movie. He'd begun to wonder what was keeping Grote, and to worry if this intruder would scare him off; then forgot all about him as the story unfolded onscreen.

A Fool There Was was pure melodrama: a tale of seduction and ruin as old as the ancient Greek theater, refined by Shakespeare, and exploited on stage and screen for a century and a half before Fox, an immigrant former candy vendor, plucked a bit player from obscurity to portray a slinky "female vampire" (abbreviated to "vamp"), obsessed with the compulsion to seduce and ruin respectable gentlemen. The thing had been done better in Edwardian times—the film creaked even more than most of its forgotten rivals from 1915—but there was no denying the presence of the female lead. Her unconventional features: The oval, almost rectangular face, Grecian nose, and enormous eyes—seduced viewers and costar alike, drawing attention away from her exaggerated gestures and over-dramatic, gliding gait, so much like a cross-country skier pushing forward through slush. In retrospect, any modern cinema-goer would find plenty there to poke fun at; but while the thing was in progress, not a single pair of eyes strayed from any scene in which she appeared.

The studio brass was unmoved, however, and released the film with as little publicity as possible, like criminals disposing of an inconvenient corpse.

Audiences were more impressed. *A Fool There Was* sold five thousand tickets in Kansas City in just one day, broke box office records across the country, and was held over in many theaters for weeks while patrons lined up around corners to see it, many not for the first time.

Amusingly, a deliberately exposed ankle aboard a ship bound for Europe was as daring as the imagery got; it was the actress's persona alone that made the gesture erotic, spurring outrage in respectable circles throughout the nation (which contributed to the receipts).

Fox didn't repeat its mistake; in fact, as each new property finished production, it inundated town and country with press releases, posters, full-page advertisements, and magazine cover stories. Much, if not all, of Bara's legacy was built squarely on the Fox publicity mill, the first over-the-top full-court press in Hollywood history, a tradition that would often match but never exceed the sheer delirious prevarication of its model.

No factoid involving the star was too outrageous: She was reincarnated from both Delilah and Lucrezia Borgia; she was born in Egypt under the shadow of the Sphinx; the name Theda Bara was an anagram of "Arab Death"; she was photographed surrounded by the skulls and skeletons of her doomed lovers, and she attended press conferences in black-curtained hotel suites accompanied by "Nubian" footmen with a white limousine parked outside.

It was all quite a journey for Theodosia Burr Goodman, born the daughter of a Jewish tailor in Cincinnati, Ohio.

Four years after it began, her career was effectively over: Dogged with legal battles with censorship authorities over the "prurient" nature of her "morality plays"; but not before she'd logged an astonishing record of forty movies and cemented her legend as the screen's first and pre-eminent Vamp with her blockbuster performance in *Cleopatra*. Ironically, the film with which she'd be forever associated vanished before the advent of "talkies" in 1927. An army of archivists had spent decades in search of a print, or even a scrap of footage: Publicity stills were all the world had to prove it ever existed. If Jasper P. Grote wasn't just blowing smoke up Valentino's skirt, the salvation of just two reels (in a condition suitable for screening) would crown a career that had basically been static since he'd dropped all nine hours of Erich von Stroheim's *Greed* back into the mainstream.

When the hapless "John Schuyler" (performed with appropriate pathos by José) had drunk himself to death after his disgrace, leaving Theda unmoved, and the lights came up, Valentino turned to the real-life vamp at his side. "How did you know where I was?"

She waited until the last straggler had wandered up the aisle. Her outfit was unconventional as always, a teal-colored gown shot through with gold lamé thread, capped with exotic shoulder pads, and cut low enough to expose a strategic sequin affixed to one breast. Crystal pendants sparkled like miniature chandeliers below her earlobes. "I almost had *Cleopatra* in Nebraska," she said. "After the deal fell through, I knew where our friend the retired cop would go next. Buster, you wouldn't notice private dicks following you day and night if they came with a brass band. When you showed up here, the rest was easy."

A sinister smile emphasized scarlet lips and kohl-rimmed eyes, the living embodiment of the illustration on the sandwich board outside the auditorium. "You should have made it *Guardians of the Galaxy* at Grauman's," she said, "but I was sure you wouldn't. I could kiss you, you fool!"

If Teddie had one fault—aside from her utter lack of scruples (which considering her abilities as a sleuth hadn't hindered her one bit)—it was her weakness for gloating. The length of the soliloquy had given Valentino the chance to gather his wits. "If you didn't like Grote's pitch in Nebraska, what makes you think things will be any different here?"

"He had the home court advantage. Now that he's in my sphere, I can get better terms. Also I wasn't sure he was legitimate. He got suspicious—I admit, once I took his bait and made the flight to hicksville, I should have dressed down to blend in with the natives—and broke things off without showing his bona fides. I guess he thought a slick character like me would stick him on the price, maybe even snatch the prize without any money changing hands."

"He's even smarter than I thought."

Which made no dent in her armor plate. "I know he slipped you a film can. It doesn't take Sherlock Holmes to guess what was in it. I sent my spies to the UCLA lab, but they couldn't find any sign that it had showed up there, so I know you smuggled it into some other place for verification somehow. You're learning; in another ten years or so you might be in my league."

Which made no dent in his own suit of mail, inferior as it was to hers. "That being the case, what did you hope to accomplish by showing up here?"

"I said I know you. You're no more likely than I am to settle for one reel when you know—or at least suspect—that you can get hold of the rest. Why else would you be here, if not to clinch the deal?"

"If you think that, it must have occurred to you that now there's no chance of Grote showing up. Once he sees you—and he probably already has—he'll be on the first flight back to Omaha."

"I doubt that. The Jasper P. Grotes of this world don't walk away from a fortune. Whatever you're paying him for that footage, you'll at least double it to snare the whole package. He can peddle it somewhere else, but it's just chickenfeed if he breaks up the set."

He took some solace in the discovery that the great Teddie Goodman had erred in assuming that the can he'd placed in the care of the LAPD was empty. She should've known better than to assume anything concerning a "lost" film. She even thought the entire film was available, not just two reels. "So what are you proposing?"

"A deal. Your budget's a joke. You can throw in with Supernova, offer a price Grote will accept, and share with us in the distribution rights."

He pretended interest in the newcomers drifting in for the next showing, but he was considering her offer. It was tempting. He didn't doubt her information: With the Turk's resources, she'd know to the penny how much the university would allow for one department's acquisition of one property, and sharing the credit (and the profits) was worth it for the opportunity to present *Cleopatra* to twenty-first-century audiences; but this woman wasn't to be trusted. If there was a way to deal Valentino and his colleagues out of the entire film, she would strike without mercy, just like the Queen of the Nile's legendary asp.

"If it's all the same to you, Teddie, I'll take my chances in the competitive market. For once you overplayed your hand; you had Scrooge McDuck's money bin at your fingertips, yet you thought you could lowball the man with something to sell. You had your chance."

Just then the lights dimmed and the vintage newsreel started unspooling, building up to Houdini's death-defying stunt high above the street. "This is where I came in," he said, rising. "Enjoy the show."

She kept her seat, legs crossed, showing a daring length of thigh through the slit in her skirt; the world had taken quite a few turns since Theda's ankle. Like her namesake, Teddie wasn't as tall as one expected of a flesh-and-blood siren; like her namesake she knew how to get around that, with strategic tailoring, eight-inch heels, and pure stubbornness of character.

"I never put all my cards on the table at once," she said. "I've got one more to play. I thought I'd hold it for another time; but this one has a sell-by date. Leo Kalishnikov's on the fence, and Dinky Schwartz won't wait forever for you to decide whether you're in or out on the Comet deal."

He froze. Once again, before he could speak, she uncrossed her legs, lifted a shining red Prada bag from the floor beside her chair, and drew something from it. "Lucky girl. Doesn't take much after her mother. These days, so much depends on looks: It's hard for a girl to get ahead with a thick waist and heavy thighs."

Valentino took the photo and studied it in the light from the screen. It was an outdoor shot of a young woman, leaning against a tree with her arms crossed in a self-conscious glamour pose. Behind her the ground sloped upward to a rock formation of some kind in the corner, somewhat out of focus. The woman wasn't as thin as Teddie—no one was, except certain supermodels—but she was much slimmer than her mother. The family resemblance, however, was unmistakable. He'd seen those same features in the snapshot Leo Kalishnikov had showed him, of the theater designer's ex-wife posing with her infant daughter.

19

HE SAT BACK down, fighting the temptation to ask more questions. Grote was officially a no-show, moving this encounter to center stage. Teddie was like a tick: Once she knew she'd gotten under your skin, there was no extricating her. She'd just dig in deeper and fester. And, skilled detective that she was, she could pretend she knew more than she did and trick her informant into giving up the rest.

But Valentino was as much of a detective as she. He knew that if he kept his mouth shut long enough, she'd spill what she had in boast. A Hollywood creature, she hungered for applause. An hour in the limelight meant as much to her as the hefty bonuses she earned in its pursuit.

He said, "You're offering to put me in touch with her in return for a seat at the bargaining table."

She leaned over and patted his hand. He recoiled from her touch, purely a reflex action. She sat back, to all appearances unoffended, and snapped her handbag shut.

"Keep the picture. You know how to get in touch with me." She uncoiled herself from her seat.

His eyes followed her up. "Giving up on Grote?"

"He spooks too easy. He'll think we're ganging up on him. He's watching us from cover right now, or I don't know my job."

And she was gone, swallowed up in the gloom of the aisle, her needle heels clicking on the concrete. They'd made no noise at all on her way in.

He studied the picture again. It was a digital printout on glossy computer stock. The tree the woman was leaning against was an evergreen; the straight trunk and rough bark were unmistakable, although the branches with their telltale needles started too high up to appear in the shot, so whether it was a spruce or a Scotch pine or a California redwood was anyone's guess. The woman's figure was trim in a one-piece outfit made of some silvery material with red piping. The picture could have been taken wherever pines and cedars grew; and was there anything less region-specific than a jogging suit? Maybe she'd never left Nebraska. That was as much as he could get out of a stationary image. He could distinguish between silver nitrate and safety stock at a glance; but that was useless here. He put away the picture.

The newsreel ended. He fidgeted, looking back over his shoulder, expecting Grote to show any second. The pause while the man (or woman) in the booth exchanged reels would be a natural time to make contact. But the feature started again. For once, the archivist was too restless to wait for the star to make her dramatic entrance. He got up, excused his way past the three people who shared his row, and went back up the aisle, turning his head this way and that in case his man had taken a seat on one side or the other; it was just like some sellers to make the customer come to them rather than the other way around. But there was no sign of that elongated head, that gangling figure folded like a wooden easel onto one of the metal chairs.

Gladys, the ticket clerk, was turning the key in the strongbox where she put the night's receipts. He asked her if anyone had been in asking for him. He described Grote.

"Nope; and I'd notice. He sounds like Pa Kettle. How was the picture?"

"Clumsy, overheated, and predictable. Loved it."

"In that case, come next week. We're showing *Nanook of the North*. You shouldn't have any trouble finding a seat."

The parking lot—its mid-century asphalt steadily being reclaimed by oat grass and vetch—was cool and dark; only the spill from the surrounding buildings shone on windshields and automobile paint. It wasn't a neighborhood for strollers that time of night. He was the only thing stirring.

Teddie had been only half right, he thought with disgust: If Grote had peeked inside the theater, he'd been put off by the discovery that Valentino wasn't alone—or worse, he'd recognized Teddie and smelled a trap. In either case, he'd left without waiting for the coast to clear. Valentino wondered if he'd found a ride.

So this was the archivist's reward for playing things by someone else's rules: An empty film can. He was the victim of a new millennial version of a snipe hunt.

Disgusted, he unlocked his car and threw himself into the driver's seat. The springs heaved beneath the sudden weight, dislodging the corpse slumped on the passenger's side. It flopped over and leaned its head on Valentino's shoulder.

20

MUCH TO HIS disenchantment, Valentino was becoming a connoisseur of police interrogation rooms. If they had a Michelin rating, he would award three stars to the one he was conducted to in East Los Angeles.

The robin's-egg blue walls smelled smartly of fresh paint, and the furniture, although built of heavy steel, was relatively comfortable: His chair accommodated his back and the tabletop was just the right height to rest his forearms on. An efficient ventilation system kept the air clear of that depressing fug of perspiration and desperation he'd come to associate with the Southern California system of justice.

He wasn't under arrest, so he'd retained his phone, which he'd used to tell Harriet that something had come up that he could discuss only in person, and would let her know when he was free. Kyle Broadhead had tried to reach him twice since he'd put in his call to the police, but he hadn't answered. It would have to do with whether a tornado had in fact struck the town of Broken Bow in 1920, leaving Grote's grandfather in possession of the first two reels of *Cleopatra*. Recent events had made that a moot point. *Some*one had found a reason to kill the man from Nebraska, even if he'd lied about having a valuable property in his possession.

Valentino had the room to himself for what felt like a season. Patently it was reserved for cooperative citizens rather than suspects in a felony: There was even a thermostat for the occupant to adjust the temperature to his liking. When a polite young patrolman asked him if he wanted anything from vending, he asked for a sandwich and a soda. The fare that came back—liverwurst and a diet Orange Crush—fell short of expectations, but the archivist devoured the meal in minutes, crumbs, dregs, and all. He'd been running all day on half a hot dog.

The lieutenant assigned to the case was named Obregon. He was dressed carefully, with a trim Gilbert Roland moustache; soft-spoken, and at least outwardly sympathetic to Valentino's plight. He had little time, however, to confirm the details in the written statement. He was called away, to return an hour and a half later with the news that the investigation was no longer his. A Homicide sergeant was on the way from the West Hollywood division of the LAPD to interview the witness. The unspoken understanding was that a sergeant from downtown outranked a lieutenant from East L.A.; but nothing in the man's manner betrayed resentment.

Valentino was no fatalist, but he was realistic about the odds of what form that substitution would assume. He barely had time for a second tour of the room—studiously ignoring the two-way mirror that covered most of one wall—when the door opened again to admit six feet of trim redhead in a green tweed suit and the iron smile of Lucille Clifford.

"YOU'RE SLOWING DOWN," she said, bumping the door shut with her hip and leaning against it, arms crossed; one hand clutched a department-issue gray cardboard folder. "It must be six months since the last time you dropped a carcass in my lap."

Did she never sleep? Aloud, he said, "Hello to you, too, Sergeant. In my defense, I was the last person on the scene that time."

"In cocktail party circles, they call that making a grand entrance." She redirected her gaze to the ceiling. "What do you call them, those bit players that keep showing up in every picture? Walk-ons?" She nodded. "Walk-ons, yeah. That's you. You get more screen time than all the stars put together."

"To be fair, so do you." He tried a smile, to defuse the tension. It felt feeble on his face.

"I *am* the star. And it's my job. What's your excuse? Never mind." She jerked her chin toward the chair on his side of the table, then joined him on the other side, spreading the folder and flicking open a pair of glasses with jade-colored frames. That was new; in all other respects, age seemed to have overlooked the sergeant. She could pose for a spread in either *Vogue* or *Guns & Ammo* without changing clothes.

Valentino recognized his signature on the printout in front of her. It was his sworn statement. She folded her hands on top of it. "You know the score by heart. Sing it again, Sam."

He gave her what he'd given Obregon, leaving out all mention of Kalishnikov and his predicament; unless and until it connected with the corpse in the car, it was a confidential matter. He brought up The Comet only because that was where he'd met the man from Nebraska. It seemed to interest her not at all.

Teddie Goodman, too, was absent from his report. The sergeant knew Supernova's shark from past experience; she wouldn't put any more store in Teddie's offer to go partners with UCLA than he had. Once that can was opened, Clifford would keep after him until she exposed Teddie's trump card—the missing daughter—and his friend's secret would become public property.

"So this fellow Grote had this *Cleopatra* movie, or claimed to," she said when he finished. "Any reason to believe it had something to do with him winding up in your car with a bullet in his chest?"

"Is that what killed him?" He'd seen no wound in the dark, had called 911 in the hope he was reporting death by natural causes. Clifford's presence had put an end to that.

"A slug in the pump will do that," she said; "close enough, this time, to singe the hair on his chest. But let's just keep that between us, okay? Our M.E.'s touchy about having the last word."

Something scampered up his spine. The shock of the corpse falling against him had catapulted him backwards, hitting the door handle and ejecting him from the car; he'd almost fallen to the ground. Sudden realization: Had the killer been crouching in his back seat, right behind him, when he sat down in front? The thought made his scalp crawl.

"You're so transparent," Clifford said. "I'd like to get you in a poker game sometime. There was almost no blood on the front seat. That means Grote was shot outside and his body dumped in the car, fully baked."

"Baked?"

"What I like to call a stiff with powder burns in the gunshot wound; I'm hoping it'll catch on. You *could* have been the one who put them there; the body was still warm when the first responders showed up. But then you might as well have signed a confession when you made the call, so I'm ruling you out for now."

"I suppose I should thank you for that."

"Don't. It isn't a favor. We're going over the ground now, looking for the spot where he was killed. Any idea how he got there, by the way? All the vehicles in the lot have been accounted for."

"The first time we met he said he'd come by Uber."

"We'll check that out; Lyft, too. Not as easy as canvassing the taxi companies and gypsy cabbies like in the old days; but we've been expecting setbacks like that ever since DNA made our job such a walk on the beach." She brushed a slender hand across the sheet in front of her. "Says here you were to contact him once you'd put that film can to the test, if it passed. Any thoughts on what he wanted to talk to you about, seeing as how the ball was in your court?"

"None whatsoever. He had no reason to back out, if that was the reason. Even if the offer was a fraud, no money had changed hands, so he wasn't guilty of a crime. And if it was genuine, he'd be expecting me to call and discuss arrangements. I doubt he got cold feet after coming halfway across the country to make his pitch. Also he didn't strike me as the nervous type. Quite the opposite."

"Kind of round-the-barn, isn't it? Why didn't he just show up at your office with the goods?"

"He didn't strike me as the trusting type either; especially since I'd been brushing him off, not knowing what he really had to sell. Paranoia goes hand-in-hand with these transactions, Sergeant. The motion-picture industry is shot through with pirates. Some pretty big names you'd think were above suspicion have been caught with their hands in the till, and the bigger the box office, the greater the temptation."

"If that's a confession, I'd rather it had to do with that corpse in the parking lot."

"I'm not that big a name; but if I were, I'd like to think I wouldn't consider myself immune to the standards of good conduct."

"That sounds stuffed-shirt enough to be true." She adjusted her glasses and turned to another page. "You don't say how that test came out. Will you turn that film can over voluntarily, or do I need to wake up a judge?"

He'd anticipated that.

"The results are inconclusive so far. We need to run more tests. The more hands it passes through—"

"That's just a variation on the same saw you've drawn before. This time we're talking about a rusty piece of tin. Don't tell me it's as delicate as old film. I've heard that lecture before. I could deliver it myself."

They were coming dangerously close to the real reason behind his excuses. If she found out the tests were being conducted using the equipment in her own department's laboratory, Harriet's job would be hanging by a thread. This was no time for his voice to quaver.

"There's no proof *Cleopatra* has anything to do with Grote's murder," he said. "He was a retired peace officer, or so he told me. Maybe his past caught up with him: a criminal he'd sent to prison, out for revenge, or a relative of the criminal's. You need more than what you've got to turn that 'rusty piece of tin' into evidence."

"You let me worry about that." She frowned at the signed statement, then flipped shut the folder and swept off the glasses. "Any thoughts on our baker, apart from your ex-con with a grudge?"

An image flashed into his mind, of a svelte figure in next season's dress; and he heard his own words to her: *You thought you could lowball the man with something to sell. You had your chance.* He wiped it from his mind.

Not fast enough. The Big Red Dog had caught the scent.

"If you're holding anything back, now's the time to come through. Otherwise . . ." She folded the glasses and tapped them on the table. They made a metallic sound, like the clang of steel doors slamming shut.

Calm. Dead calm.

"You've got everything, Sergeant."

Clifford called in the polite young officer.

"Take Mr. Valentino home. His car's in the impound."

Riding in the back seat of a police cruiser for the second time that morning, he felt more like a prisoner than he had under the sergeant's interrogation: Cloistered behind wire-reinforced Plexiglas between doors without handles, bulletproof windows separating him from the colorful Rivera-esque murals they were passing. He thought how unlikely it was that Teddie would have had anything to do with Grote's murder. Unlikely? Preposterous!

But she had been on the scene, as had Valentino. And he remembered something Broadhead had once said: "If Teddie wants something bad enough, she'll go after it, if it means climbing using the rib cage of your skeleton for a ladder."

21

"IS IT MY birthday?"

Hastily, Valentino sat up in bed, smoothing the covers across his lap to make room for the footed tray Harriet had brought to his bedside. The dishes were covered and a crisp napkin rested in a silver holder. He took sly satisfaction from evidence that the evenings he'd exposed her to Cary Grant and Greer Garson had borne fruit. The slope of the sunlight coming through the east window told him the morning was almost gone.

"You haven't been asleep quite *that* long," she said, arranging the tray across his middle. "Before you tie into the egg whites and turkey bacon, you might want to read the late-breaking news. It might upset your indigestion." She drew a sleek tablet from the tray's side pocket (designed, appropriately, to hold a traditional newspaper), tapped a key, swiped the screen, and handed it to him.

It was the online edition of *Los Angeles Times*, where a familiar face smiled out from three columns of text; it was always a shock to come across himself looking back at him from anything other than a mirror. The unaccustomed evening dress told him the picture had been taken at the grand opening of The Oracle, and somewhat clumsily cropped so that a hand (he forgot just whose) rested on his right shoulder with no arm visibly attached; some bleary-eyed employee in composition had made hasty work of it in order to meet the deadline. It was headed:

UCLA ARCHIVIST QUESTIONED IN APPARENT HOMICIDE

"Just how long *did* I sleep?" he said. "No paper's broken a story this fast since *The Front Page.*"

"Simmer down, Jimmy Olsen. Boys don't cry 'Extra, extra' in the street anymore. You can post a story worldwide before an old-time linotypist finishes cracking his knuckles."

He read swiftly. Grote was identified as a retired Midwestern lawman, his death attributed to a gunshot in East L.A. Valentino didn't make another appearance until the final paragraph, where he was said to have been identified as a witness. Details were scanty. There was no mention of *Cleopatra.*

"The headline makes me sound like a suspect. My God, is there a CNN crew camped out outside?" He still had occasional flashbacks of the media circus surrounding the first time his activities had put him in contact with a corpse.

"Oh, please. If the *Times* didn't happen to have art on you in a soup-and-fish they wouldn't have bothered to run the story until the paper edition. Lead with the national debt, finish with *Hägar the Horrible,* and tuck you in the middle, like the sorbet between the clam chowder and the rack of lamb: Fluff for the shut-ins who read the bridge column."

He took one last look at the picture—*Just what are you grinning about?*—and gave her back the tablet. "It was sweet of you not to pump me for information last night."

"You were wiped out. Fish in a barrel." She drew a chair

up to the bed and sat. "Now that you've slept on it, give me what you got over the fruit cup." She crossed her legs; a gesture which, dressed as she was in brushed jeans, sandals, and a short-sleeved top, carried all the allure of Teddie Goodman in her Saks originals, with none of the transparent cunning that went into their selection.

He spoke in bursts, plowing through the chunks of pear, melon, and pineapple, then Harriet's healthy alternatives to scrambled eggs, bacon, and toast in between; after two days of chasing leads, both his dining and sleeping habits were part of a dimly remembered past. This time, he reported the conversation with Teddie, which he'd withheld from the sergeant; as much of it as he felt safe disclosing even in this company.

Harriet was silent for a disturbing length of time. Then:

"That wasn't her whole pitch. She's a lot of things—most of them unmentionable in terms of a PG-13 rating—but she's not clumsy. She wouldn't scuff her Jimmy Choos on the streets of East L.A. with a deal she knew you wouldn't go for. You and she, working together? Let's start with something inside the realm of possibility; like an end to the Marvel Universe in our lifetime."

The alarm clock on the nightstand read 11:06. "Aren't you late for work?"

"Graveyard shift; no pun intended or appreciated. Chum, you know that under this roof you get to change the subject just once every six months, same as the batteries in the smoke detector. You've used it up for this year."

He put his head back against the pillow and closed his eyes. "Clifford didn't buy it either, I could tell."

Then he told her everything, beginning with Kalishnikov's secret origins, his old trouble with the law, the blackmail scheme, and finally the photograph Teddie had dealt like an ace from her sleeve. Harriet asked where it was.

"Jacket pocket. Wherever that is."

His Bruins warm-up jacket happened to be hanging on the back of her chair. She hooked it around in front of her, patted the pockets, and drew out the picture. She glanced at it, then turned it his direction. "You saw the one she took with her mother. Any resemblance?"

"To the mother. All babies look like Otto Preminger."

"Remind me not to discuss children with you." She fanned herself with the photo. "You know, I suspected something when that B-movie Cossack brought borscht in a Tupperware dish to the grand opening. That was laying it on with a steam shovel." She stopped fanning and frowned. "Do you think Teddie—?"

"No! Lie, cheat, steal, sure; Kyle would say put it in Latin and you'll find it in her family crest. Murder?" It was his turn to frown. "Maybe, if her bag of tricks ever ran out, though I doubt that too. Anyway, why kill Grote, if he was her only chance to nab *Cleopatra*? She wouldn't have brought out that picture if she had what she wanted."

"Clifford told you the body was still warm when the uniforms got there. How do you know she didn't run into him after she met you, and killed him when he wouldn't hand over the film? He had to have some reason to set up that meeting with you. Maybe he'd decided to close the deal, knowing your sterling reputation for always following through on a transaction."

Valentino did his best to ape Sergeant Clifford's expression when he'd delivered his incomplete account of his midnight adventure.

Harriet lifted a shoulder and let it drop. "Yeah, okay. But it doesn't mean she's in the clear. That's Clifford's headache. You need to give your fifty-foot woman the rest of the story."

"I can't. It would look like I was exploiting a tragedy to take Teddie out of the competition."

"The sergeant's a smart cookie. She cut you slack for a rea-

son. The longer you keep your mouth shut, the worse it will be
when she finds out Teddie was there. Notice I said 'when,' not
'if'; that walking mannequin sticks out like radioactive waste.
And Clifford holds the department record for busts that stay
busted.

"You want to spend a year in San Quentin for withholding
evidence in a homicide?" she went on. "The trusty who books
their movies is a fan of the Hallmark Channel."

He made a face. "That last part was low."

"Thanks. I've been saving it. So what's your answer?"

"I'll think about it. Seriously," he added, when she gave him
that look. "What news from the lab?"

She hung on to the expression a moment longer; but she could
never resist talking shop, especially when she knew that in cases
like this his eyes wouldn't glaze over when she got technical.

"My specialist owes me a solid for saving his butt over one
of those errors *I'm* a specialist in. So far, he's found nothing
to indicate that can isn't what Grote claimed it was. My guy
moonlights at the county art museum. He saved the gallery a
bundle last year when he found aluminum shavings imbedded
in a 'newly discovered' Botticelli, who died three hundred years
before the metal went into production; seems the forger kept
his studio above a cookware factory."

"He should've been a filmmaker. They never get caught."

She continued as if he hadn't interrupted. "The can is the
standard type used during the period in question—of course
you knew that, or you wouldn't have bothered to bring it home—
and the ink used in the stenciling—tannins, ferrous sulfate, pine
tar, and other natural compounds—went out of fashion when
synthetics came in. No modern contaminants so far. You don't
catch a break like finding Reynolds Wrap in an old master twice.

"Of course," she said, "someone who knows what he's doing

could conceivably get access to the original materials. That art forger managed to recreate pigments commonly used during the Renaissance."

"Any trace of camphor or silver nitrate inside? Guncotton?"

"He's still working on the outside. These things take time; and it isn't as if he hasn't anything else on his plate, like a triple homicide in Burbank. Authenticating a tin can—an empty one at that—doesn't rate high on the list of priorities, especially when the brass can't know about it."

"Still, it's encouraging."

"Encouraging doesn't make the case in court. More tests to go. Unfortunately, we won't know anything for sure until one of those tests proves it to be a fake. It's like a vasectomy: The cat's out of the bag only when the stick turns pink. Sorry, Val."

"If it is a fake, why go to all that trouble? There was no deal until Grote produced those reels."

"Maybe the whole thing was just an excuse to get close to you, as a Kalishnikov contact. Anybody who did his homework on you knows what bait to use. If the film doesn't exist, your first idea, that he was in on the blackmail, is the only alternative that would convince a jury."

"Saturday Night at the Movies" rescued him from responding. The music was coming from his jacket in Harriet's lap. He got hold of it before she could snatch it away, fished out his cell, and answered it.

"People usually answer my calls," said the dry voice on the other end.

"Kyle. I had a busy night."

"I know. I can read. I wanted to tell you that tornado yarn checked out: What today we'd call an EF-Four. It took out three blocks, including the Roxy Theater in May nineteen-twenty. But that's water under the bridge now, isn't it? Whoever killed

Jasper Grote put the seal of approval on his story. Of course, if you've got those reels in hand—"

"I didn't kill him, Kyle."

"I'm disappointed. I wanted to ask if Theda's thighs are as chubby in a toga as they looked in *The Unchastened Woman*."

"Can we talk about this later? I'll fill you in, promise." *Except on all things Kalishnikov.*

Broadhead's tone changed. "Are you all right?"

Harriet, who'd been listening, took the phone from Valentino's hand. "For God's sake, you old humbug, queue up *Steel Magnolias* and give the man a chance to rest."

"Hello, Harriet. It's been too—"

She hit END.

III

A GOODMAN
IS HARD TO FIND

22

THEY DECIDED TO spend the day unwinding at Knott's Berry Farm. They'd take Harriet's car, as Valentino's was still in police custody. He was dressing in preparation for hours of wandering among the amusements (he never tired of the western holdups staged along the narrow-gauge railroad; she favored the alligator farm across the street) when Dinky Schwartz called, asking him to stop by his construction project downtown. He wanted to show him something.

The archivist asked for a raincheck, explaining his plans.

"Perfect! It's right on your way. If your lady friend likes you, she'll love this."

He clamped the phone to his chest and passed the news to Harriet, who'd changed into shorts and a tennis top. She processed the information, fixing the strap of her sun visor to accommodate a ponytail; then smiled. "He's worth meeting, just for his name."

THE WIND WAS blowing out to sea, lowering the ozone threat, and the sun shone bright on the iconic billboard on

Sunset. Liam Neeson's face seemed to be squinting against the glare.

No progress had been made on Jubilación Arms ("a place for seniors to reside in seventy stories of dignity and luxury") beyond a few tons of displaced earth, currently being pushed into new Play-Doh shapes by yellow bulldozers. But Valentino had been an Angelino long enough to learn how quickly a lingering demolition site could sprout into a bristle of steel and stone; whole neighborhoods became unrecognizable overnight. Like the world of Norse mythology, his adopted hometown was constantly being destroyed and resurrected—if not newer and better than before, then at least as permanent; until the next time.

The contractor, red-faced and bulky as ever, had shed his coveralls and hard hat in favor of slacks, a Dodgers ball cap, and a Hawaiian shirt big enough to host a luau. His gap-toothed grin broadened to the creaking point when he took Harriet's hand in a paw the size of a platter. "Miss, I don't know why your fella bothers to put on any clothes when he goes out. Nobody'd be looking at him."

"I would." Her smile—adjusted for mouth-to-face ratio—was as wide.

Valentino said, "Excuse the bluntness. She weighs brains for a living."

Dinky's eyes sparkled; a universal phenomenon whenever a pair rested on the CSI (so long as they belonged to a male; although not necessarily). "We've got a thing or two in common. It's not all mud and mortar with me. My crew dug up a human torso last year in Capistrano. Had a tattoo of a mermaid on it."

She tended to snort when she laughed unexpectedly; for some reason it never seemed to put anyone off. "I worked that one! The arms and legs turned up in a dumpster in my jurisdiction. We're still looking for the head."

"I'll keep an eye out. I got a dozen excavations going between here and Tijuana." He slung an arm like a side of beef across Valentino's shoulders. "Let's go out back. You're gonna want to see this."

"I just hope it's not a head."

Dinky held the door for them to step out onto the treated-wood porch and led the way down the steps and around behind the trailer. There, what looked like a huge black plastic tarp had been spread out on the ground, anchored at the corners by broken pieces of cinder block. It seemed to take up an acre of ground. On the other side of this lounged a pair of young workers thumbing cell phones. Stencils on their hard hats and patches on their coveralls read D. SCHWARTZ CONTRACTORS, INC. At a signal from Dinky they holstered their phones and stooped to remove the weights from the corners. That done, they stood facing their employer, arms bent at their sides. Valentino, who recognized a rehearsed scene when he saw one, smiled at his old friend's weakness for theatrics.

Dinky milked the moment. "I spent more time researching this one thing than I did the four housing tracts I built in San Berdoo five years ago; burned up fifteen tanks of gas—with a war on in oil country, mind—and wore out three pairs of boots pounding asphalt and concrete and a prairie dog town in Bakersfield. If there was so much as one speaker post still standing anywhere in the Golden State, I went there, measured the ground, grilled the grandson of the last guy to pop the corn; you name it, I did it, and I found out plenty, most of it disappointing as hell.

"This old world's hard on outdoor enterprise," he went on. "Wood rots, concrete freezes and cracks, steel's dear, and aluminum only holds up when the Santa Anas aren't blowing. Where do you think I finally found just what I needed? Camper's World! I only stopped in the place to use the toilet. They were running a sale on inflatable mattresses; which is nothing new, but they're better than back in my hiking days. I spent my share of time blowing 'em up manually, as heaven forbid I should sleep on the ground like Daniel Boone. It's a miracle I didn't blow an artery. Nowadays you can save your breath, on account of they inflate themselves.

"Well, when I saw what they had for sale, I told my bladder to keep its shirt on. Couldn't wait to get back to the office. I put my design-and-development guys on it right away. They whipped this out in ten days."

This was all so much Greek. Valentino had never known his old friend to be garrulous; back in school, when Broadhead had called for a response from the class, Dinky had ducked for cover behind a copy of the professor's own *Persistence of Vision*.

Thinking of Broadhead reminded him that he and Harriet had an appointment with Kyle and Fanta later; their schedule was growing tight. He checked the time. "Dink—?" He gestured with the phone.

The contractor grinned, his broad face flushing a deeper shade of crimson; here was the old shy Dinky, embarrassed by his own enthusiasm. He nodded at his crew. Each man picked up a cord that looked like a plastic clothesline and gave it a smart yank.

An electric motor started thumping, accompanied by a sound like compressed air filling a tire. Gradually—at first infinitesimally—the wrinkles in the tarp began to flatten out, the depressions between them to fill. Thirty seconds of this, and then the whole expanse took on a third dimension, the surface lifting from the ground; Valentino thought of a hot-air balloon acquiring shape. It opened like an enormous book, exposing a pristine white surface that had been folded inside.

Now he knew what he was looking at.

An inert thing only minutes before, it towered above the ground, the witnesses, then the trailer, spreading right and left as it climbed, filling the lot from side to side. By the time the motor sputtered to a stop, Dinky, Valentino, and the hard hats—who had come around to their side to watch the show—were looking up at a vast motion-picture screen, blazing white, as wide as a football field and as high as a two-story building.

Valentino felt Harriet's arm around his waist, the thrill in her body. She was a sucker for any kind of fireworks. Well, so was he.

"Can't beat it." Dinky's voice dripped with awe. (And he had known what to expect!) "And it deflates just as quick. You can store it in a shed between showings, out of the elements, so it lasts years and years, come whatever Mother Nature decides to throw at it. Think of it, Val! If all the buildings in L.A. were built like this, the mayor could push a button, flatten the place from Santa Monica to San Clemente, wait for the all-clear, then pump it back up and blow a big fat juicy raspberry at the Big One!"

"Provided he got everyone out in time," Valentino said; "but I see what you mean. It's wonderful, Dink. And cost-effective. You could put up four screens for the price of one."

"Four?" Even his think-big friend was a step behind him.

"A multiplex drive-in! You couldn't have done it back in the days of detachable speakers; they'd be competing against each other. But the FCC has radio bands to spare. You can channel *Top Gun* to one frequency, *Pride and Prejudice* to another, roll up the windows, and never have to worry about fighter jets drowning out Jane Austen. Four times the revenue every night."

Suddenly he realized they were veering dangerously close to a monetary discussion. He glanced again at his phone.

"I have to go. Thanks for the demonstration. Congratulations, old buddy! You could be the next Darryl Zanuck."

But Dinky looked embarrassed. "Uh, Val—"

Here it comes.

"This glorified beach toy set me back ten thousand, clear out of pocket. I couldn't dip into company funds without getting in Dutch with the bank, which isn't exactly high on adventurous investment. I need up-front revenue. I'm out on a limb here without a John Hancock—yours or your friend Khrushchev's, or whatever he calls himself—on that contract."

"About that—"

"Understand," he broke in, "it's my lawyers got my head on the block. This murder business I've been reading about—"

"It's got nothing to do with this, Dink; or with me. I was in the wrong place at the wrong time, that's all."

"Happens more often than you'd think," Harriet put in.

Valentino gave her a look that said *You're not helping*. To Schwartz: "Don't worry about it."

The big face smoothed out. "If you say so, okay." Then it puckered again. "Um, when do you think—?"

Harriet's arm tightened around his waist.

"Soon, Dink. I promise."

Hands were shaken all around, and they left. Buckling himself into the passenger seat, Valentino felt her eyes on him. "Not now, okay?"

"I didn't say anything." She started the car.

23

THEY HAD A long-standing date to celebrate Kyle and Fanta Broadhead's wedding anniversary. The couple—Fanta, actually, who was in charge of all arrangements in the Broadhead household—had moved up the dinner reservation to accommodate Harriet's changed hours downtown. They met at the front desk in The Divine Comedy, L.A.'s newest restaurant specializing in Northern Italian cuisine. It was still turning away customers who assumed it was a training stable for stand-up comics.

Instead of the usual scenic murals, all the rooms were decorated with Renaissance-style frescoes based on classic dramas set in Italy. Their private chamber showcased a scene from *Two Gentlemen of Verona*. The titular figures stood glaring at each other in a palazzo.

Fanta, a strapless black cocktail dress accentuating her slim figure, lowered her voice to a confidential level. "When Val told him what he was working on, Mr. Romance here wanted to switch to the *Antony and Cleopatra* room. That's the one with the double-suicide. I told him it was booked."

"Was it?" Harriet smiled.

"Immaterial. Then he switched to the assassination scene from *Julius Caesar*. I convinced him all that blood would clash with the Alfredo sauce."

"Youth is so squeamish. You'd think a steady diet of *Game of Thrones* would strengthen its stomach." The Bohemian Broadhead looked uncomfortable in a charcoal-gray suit cut specially to his thick frame—one of his child bride's improvements.

Harriet said, "Change of subject, please. In a couple of hours I'll be up to my neck in entrails."

Fanta nudged Valentino. "We should switch partners. How'd we ever wind up with these ghouls?"

"You moved to L.A." Her husband held her chair while she sat. To Valentino: "How was the Farm? Did you pan for gold, and if so is the night on you?"

"We got there too late. It was all panned out." Valentino took a seat across from Harriet, who'd changed into a blue frock with a square neckline that set off her elegant collarbone. "And the night *is* on me. I bet Harriet you two wouldn't last six months."

"I bet Fanta three," Broadhead said. "We're splitting dessert."

As host, Valentino tried to keep the focus on the happy couple, but inevitably the conversation turned to his activities of the past twenty-four hours—and stayed there from the antipasto through the gelato. He held out only as far as the salad.

In as few words as possible he explained his business with Leo Kalishnikov—leaving the theater designer's Russian imposture in favor of his entanglement in an old criminal case and the spectre of blackmail—and ended with the grisly discovery in Valentino's car outside the underground theater. Tying Leo in to two murders struck him as less of a betrayal than if he were to expose what was after all a mild case of self-advertisement. One entanglement was personal, and sacred; the other a matter of public record.

Plainly, the Broadheads were dissatisfied, and suspicious, so he pushed on without pause to Henry Anklemire's memories of "Aunt Theo," Teddie Goodman's surprise visit to The Priest's Hole, and Sergeant Clifford's entry into the melodrama. Surprisingly enough, he finished all this before the coffee arrived.

"So that's what's waiting for you back at the office," Fanta said to Harriet, after a brief silence broken only by the tinkling of spoons in cups. "I suppose running a paraffin test on Teddie's hands would be a waste of time; she's seen enough whodunits, and gunpowder's no match for plain old soap and water."

"We haven't used paraffin since *Dragnet*," Harriet said. "Anyway, it's not important. Val left her out."

"Yes, he's good at that." Broadhead blew on his cup.

Fanta rescued the party from an awkward pause. "I wouldn't want to be in your boyfriend's shoes when the sergeant finds out."

"The lad has a soft spot for Teddie," Broadhead said. "She's the stone on which he whets his blade. But I'm just as inclined to rule her out as a suspect."

"You?" Valentino was shocked. "Wasn't it you who said she got up one morning on the wrong side of the coffin?"

"Don't get me wrong; she thinks the Seven Deadly Sins is a bucket list. But she wouldn't sink to something so mundane as plugging a man with a bullet when she has so many other spells in her book; that would be bad form. I'd look everywhere else first. If this Grote had one dirty iron in the fire—extortion or fraud, one's as good as the other—he had several, one of which was bound to catch up with him eventually, without any assistance from our fatal fashion plate.

"Val was born under an unlucky star," he said, addressing the table. "Look at the record: Sooner or later, every Sweeney Todd in Greater Los Angeles can be depended upon to dump the result of his handiwork in his lap."

Fanta patted his forearm. "Remind me to offer you second chair at his trial. We'll enter his horoscope into evidence and plead not guilty by reason of cosmic interference."

"You're a copyright attorney. What do you know of criminal law?" Broadhead added cream to his coffee. "Maybe there's a precedent: The United States v. God."

"Dinner *and* a show," Valentino said; "with blasphemy as an added attraction. So glad to have entertained you all with the prospect of my imminent incarceration."

"Worry-wart! Clifford has a crush on you or she'd have locked you up and thrown away the key all the other times she fell over you at the scene of a crime. *Cleopatra*'s what we need to focus on. Are we any closer to it than we were in the beginning?"

"Farther than ever, Kyle. I'm starting to think that film can was a Trojan horse; just the trinket I could be expected to jump on, putting Grote within striking range of Kalishnikov. Maybe he wasn't a blackmailer at all; just one of those Old Testament cops, obsessed with justice. Maybe his grandfather really *was* a bike messenger who rescued a rusty hunk of tin from a tornado. Grote found it among the family possessions and the whole shady deal sprang from there."

"Well, that's disappointing," Fanta said. "Aren't mysteries supposed to come with solutions? I thought it was a package deal."

"Not in Hollywood." Broadhead, determined to create the perfect blend, emptied a packet of sugar into his cup. "We put answers up on the screen and keep our murderers to ourselves."

Their waiter chose that moment to appear. He was a curly-headed youth who looked like Dionysus. "Is everything all right?" He stammered a little.

"What a presumptuous question," Broadhead said. We were talking of homicide."

The young man took himself away.

Harriet raised a glass. "Happy first anniversary. What's the proper gift, paper?"

"Taken care of," Fanta said. "Kyle gave me his manuscript to read."

Broadhead leaned over to Valentino and whispered past his hand. "Obviously she hasn't gotten to page eighty-seven."

"What's that?" Hers were the youngest ears at the table.

Broadhead held out his hand to Valentino. "Let's see that photo."

Fanta said, "Hang on! What's on page eighty-seven?"

"I don't want to spoil the ending. The photo." He waggled his fingers.

Valentino wasn't sure at first if he'd transferred the picture Teddie had given him to his sportcoat. He had. He drew it out and passed it across the table.

Broadhead spent a minute moving a pair of readers forward and back without unfolding them, magnifying-lens fashion. "She's built like a trapeze artist." He studied the picture another minute, then returned it. "How long have you lived in California?"

"Half my life."

"Which is just long enough to change the batteries in my smoke detector; but long enough to know your way around. If you spent more time sightseeing and less time counting anachronisms in *The Ten Commandments*, you'd recognize a local landmark when you stub your toe on it. It's worse, come to think of it: You've seen *Rebel Without a Cause* how many times? Here." He held out his glasses.

"I don't need those."

"Obviously you do."

Valentino passed them around the image, finishing on the blurred patch in the upper left-hand corner. What he'd taken for a line of boulders was in fact man-made. Now he recognized the three domes sharing a stretch of architecture a hundred yards up the slope from Carla Schmeisser, Kalishnikov's daughter. Trees like the one she was leaning against grew in all the city's parks like grass; but only one contained such a structure.

"The Griffith Observatory!"

Broadhead nodded. "In the Hills! If whoever took the picture had stepped back ten paces, he'd have gotten the Hollywood sign.

"What do you think, Mr. Film Detective?" he said. "Is it coincidence that two native Nebraskans should wander into your own backyard at the very time your drive-in partner—yet another alumnus of America's corn patch—is being harassed with the details of his past there?"

"What's a Russian doing in a corn patch anyway?" Fanta put in. "I thought their thing was wheat."

Harriet recovered the ball. "I was raised in Yreka. The place was crawling with shirttail Romanovs whose great-grandparents came there on the lam from the October Revolution. My Papa Johansen went looking for work when he finished cutting down all the timber in Sweden. Everyone here came from somewhere else, if you go far enough back. What about the Broadheads, Kyle? Yorkshire?"

"North Dakota, actually." The professor seemed once again to be turning over something Valentino had said—or rather what he hadn't—but returned to the subject at hand. "The observatory isn't on the way to anywhere. Unless you're a mountainclimber, there's no other reason to go. Our wandering daughter has an interest in astronomy. I'd start right here at home, with the stargazers among the UCLA faculty."

Valentino frowned. "That's a stretch. Maybe she just got tired of standing in Lana Turner's footprints at Grauman's and of doing all the other touristy stuff in town and just wound up there, maybe to make out with whoever took her picture."

Harriet squeezed his hand.

"Spare me the autobiographical details," grumped Broadhead. "I've lived here most of my life and I've never been within a mile of the place; yet I recognized it and you didn't. Fanta?"

"I was born here; and the answer is me neither."

"*I've* been," Valentino said. "Twice, in fact."

Broadhead shook his head.

"You don't count. You only went there to convene with James Dean's troubled shade." He pointed his fork at the picture Valentino was still holding. "Her, too, possibly; which if true would make your job easier. You only have to look in our own department to pick up the trail of a *paisan*."

"Or you could ask Teddie where she got the picture," Harriet said.

The others laughed.

She looked hurt. "The obvious needed to be stated, is all."

"The shortest distance between Teddie and the truth is a corkscrew," said Broadhead. "She played that card to tease Val into accepting her terms. The police could book her as a material witness, but only as long as it took Turkus' attorneys to show up with a writ."

"Suppose I find Carla Schmeisser," Valentino said. "What then? I should ask if she was in cahoots with Jasper Grote, they fell out, and she shot him, then parked the body in my car hoping to implicate me?

"Two birds, one stone. The math never gets simpler."

"*Any*way," Fanta said, her hand again on her husband's arm, "isn't finding Carla what you've been engaged to do? The thing that would discharge your obligation and spare you another brush with bankruptcy on the Comet deal? If I were you, I'd hope she had nothing to do with Grote. That would leave solving his murder up to the police, and incidentally get you off the hook with Sergeant Clifford—once you've come clean."

"You mean lay it all on Teddie Goodman."

"As much as you admire her," Broadhead said, "why not?"

Fanta said, "Seriously, what's on page eighty-seven?"

24

HARRIET, STILL FACING a full shift, confined her drinking to one toast. By the others' standards, it was a fairly alcoholic evening: Even Kyle, who contained his vices to a daily pipe of tobacco, finished his coffee and nursed a tablespoonful of cognac in a balloon glass over the crepes. The Broadheads left by Uber, as they had come, and Harriet dropped Valentino off at her apartment on the way to work.

As often happened when he imbibed, the archivist slept without dreaming and woke up with someone clog-dancing in his head and the urge to dive into a tank of ice water and drink it to the bottom. When music started playing and he connected it to his phone, he had to take it in both hands to lift it off the nightstand; his fingers were as numb as wooden clothespins. When a phone rang, his inborn camera moved in for a close-up. The voice of a circus barker greeted him from the other end.

"Hey, I got you out of bed! I'm sorry as hell, Professor! I eat when I'm hungry and sleep when I'm sleepy, which is almost never. Geezerhood has its points."

"'S'okay, Henry. Just don't yell." He propped himself up against the head of the bed. The room was gray; either the sun had yet to come up or the wind had changed, bringing with it the smog for a return engagement. "What time *is* it?"

"You tell me. The battery in my watch died same day as George Burns. Listen, I'm moving out of my dump end of the month. Some pencil-jockey in Sacramento thinks we ain't got enough superhighways in this town and it turns out I'm sitting on the interchange."

"I'm sorry." Which was true. Valentino missed his cozy projection booth.

"Hey, I'm used to wandering in the desert. I don't need this much space anyway, and I can't see shoving half this crap I got into a U-Haul just to put it in storage."

"If you're asking me to help you move—"

"Naw, I got a nephew. There's something here might interest you; wouldn't of thought of it except for what we talked about yesterday. Can I bring it to your office later?"

Valentino looked at his screen: 5:11 A.M. "What is it?"

"Well, if I was to describe it over the phone, you might not want it. You'll want to see it in person."

One of the less ominous remarks he'd heard lately; but still . . .

"Can it wait till ten? Assuming you can tell time by then?"

"I can get that from the operator."

Henry Anklemire hung up before Valentino could tell him that was no longer possible. He stumbled into the bathroom, drank straight from the tap, and went back to bed. By the time he rose he'd forgotten all about the conversation.

THE RELENTLESS RUTH caught him on his way past her desk, waving a message torn off her self-censored memo pad. It told him he had a package out for delivery by the United States Postal Service and that it would arrive before 5 P.M.

"Didn't they say what it was?" he said. "I'm not expecting anything."

She shrugged and said nothing. On some rare occasions the old dragon avoided commentary of any kind; a sort of fasting period while she cleansed herself of the poisons brought on by a workplace unworthy of loyalty. Valentino lived for those days.

It wasn't until he laid the message atop the pile on his own desk that he remembered vaguely that he *did* have a package of some kind coming; another half hour passed before his hangover subsided enough to bring back the circumstances of his early-morning conversation with Anklemire. He hoped it wasn't some ungainly piece of furniture. If the little flack's taste in décor matched his sartorial preferences, it would clash with everything else in the archivist's life.

Three cups of coffee from the wheezing vending machine in the hallway restored sufficient of his faculties to place the calls he'd planned. The results weren't really disappointing, because he hadn't expected anything to come of them. No one in UCLA's astronomy department would admit to having heard of anyone named Carla Schmeisser; although it seemed everyone he spoke to was preoccupied with some new astral phenomenon and not really paying attention. One let slip they were tracking what they hoped was a previously undiscovered comet.

Comet. He hoped it was a good omen. This adventure was perilously low on those.

He scanned the photograph Teddie Goodman had given him and sent it to all his likely contacts, but the woman posing in Griffith Park near the observatory failed to ring bells. His friends in film preservation couldn't help either. Their apologies, at least, sounded sincere; but a polite dead end is still a dead end. Evidently Broadhead's hunch was wrong: Valentino's quarry wasn't star-struck, either by the delights of the Milky Way or by the charms of James Dean.

He sat drumming his fingers against his chin, trying to summon fresh inspiration, when Ruth broke her fast.

He recognized that howl: Someone had passed her guard post without waiting to be announced. There was only one creature on the campus with that kind of *Chutzpah*; he and the receptionist belonged to incompatible species. A fist beat a tattoo on his door.

"Come in, Henry!" He got up.

The little man swept in, clutching something bulky under one arm. Today he was nearly unrecognizable in dull gray sweats and scruffy sneakers. The clothes truly made this man: Absent his trademark loud checks, hand-painted neckties, and complete lack of color-sense, he left almost no impression at all. Valentino suspected that under the Phillies baseball cap was nothing but naked scalp, unadorned by any of the toupees he scored at studio auctions.

Anklemire picked up on his reaction.

"I took a personal day. That chili I ate yesterday ought to come with a HazMat sticker. Guess you're not used to seeing me all dressed down."

"Are you sure you should be up and about?" He did look paler than usual; quite a feat, considering he spent most of his working days wheeling and dealing in a basement office next to the boiler.

"No worries. I chugged a bottle of Maalox for breakfast. But I brung a relief pitcher just in case." He hauled a squat brown vessel from a pocket. An Aztec scowled out from the Spanish label with a face carved from red sandstone. "Good luck finding this stuff on the 'net. The village where I get it don't even have a name. You have to drive down in person, and you have to know a guy. I can fix you up."

"Some other time."

"If you're worried about getting it past the border—"

"You know a guy, yes. I'm a little busy, Henry, so if we can—"

"Oh, sure!" He put away the bottle and removed the burden from under his arm.

It was an ancient leather briefcase, scuffed orange at the corners and secured with a single strap and a giant safety pin with a pink cap on the clasp. He set it atop one of the heaps on the desk (a particularly brittle assortment of vintage press kits), undid the pin, and reached in with both hands to retrieve something wrapped in blue tissue. Valentino cleared a space for him to set it down.

With awkward delicacy, the PR agent spread the tissue and lifted out something that shimmered like spun gold in the fluorescent light.

It was a thick fold of fabric, indisputably old, the rich liquid brown of Turkish coffee. A smell of camphor filled the room, but also an odor both subtle and pervasive. It suggested bustling bazaars in far-off places that hadn't existed since the fall of the Ottoman Empire; places Valentino knew only from the silver screen. He thought of exotic spices, strong tobacco, old silk.

"Feel!" Anklemire slid the bundle his way.

Valentino stroked it cautiously, as he would a strange dog. It was butter-soft and nearly weightless when he lifted a fold. It seemed to have been woven from the fleece of some extinct breed of goat.

He snatched back his hand, as if he'd been caught profaning a holy relic.

"Theda Bara's shawl!"

Anklemire nodded, and went on nodding as if he'd forgotten to stop. He was a living bobblehead doll.

"The one I told you about, remember? She'd sashay around in it, flapping her arms and chattering in that deep voice she had. It meant a lot to her, don't know why. Maybe she wore it in a movie or slept under it with Tom Mix."

"You've had it all these years? How—?"

"It's been in the back of a linen closet since I moved in. I clean forgot all about it till yesterday. Digging it out—well, it sent me back. When I told Aunt Theo we were moving back East and she wouldn't be my babysitter no more, she said she wanted to give me something: "to remember your old *Bubele* by," that's what she said. She was Jewish too, you know; that Arab story was beeswax. Sometimes I think that's how I came by my calling.

"Anyway, I guess I made an impression. I never pestered her about being an old-time movie star, maybe that was it. She never talked about the old days, so I guess she'd had her fill."

"What's this?"

Reaching out again, Valentino touched a reddish-brown patch that had caught his eye. It didn't match the rest of the material and was crusty to the touch.

Anklemire looked sheepish.

"Yeah, she apologized for that. She said she couldn't do anything about it on account of it was so old it would fall apart at the cleaners. It's blood."

25

VALENTINO LET GO of the shawl, unconsciously wiping his hand on his shirt, just as if the blood were still fresh. Hollywood's history was sanguinary enough without a previously undiscovered murder in its past.

Anklemire read the reaction. "Not to worry, Professor. Nobody croaked in it. Auntie Theo said she stuck herself once pinning it on, but she just couldn't bring herself to part with it before. Heck, I was a rough-and-tumble kid; I bet she used up a gallon of iodine on me, all the times I scraped a knee playing stickball. She knew a little schmutz wouldn't spook me." His face lit up. "Hey, maybe you brainiacs can use the DNA to clone another Theda Bara."

The archivist made a pained face; but for some reason what the little man had said struck a dull chord somewhere in his subconscious. It was brief, and left no echo. Lately, it seemed, he was experiencing more than his share of those moments.

"Thank you, Henry." He tried to sound sincere. There was a time such a gift would have thrilled him, but that was before The Oracle drained his finances, forcing him to sell off the many one-of-a-kind artifacts he'd accumulated from motion-picture sets long gone to the wrecking ball. With each item lost to eBay and brick-and-mortar auction houses, the sting had faded, leaving him with no regret for the loss of his collection; in fact, he'd felt a sense of liberation from the senseless accumulation of material things. They had begun to own *him* rather than the other way around.

Still, he couldn't stop himself from reaching out once again to stroke a garment that had swaddled a film legend. He was like a recovering alcoholic who suddenly found himself holding a bottle of good Scotch. He withdrew his hand a third time and tucked it behind his back with the other, safely out of reach.

"Are you sure you want to part with it?"

"Tell you the truth, I don't know why I hung on to it this long. If it'd make you feel better, give me a plug onscreen for pushing the Cleo flick: You can stick it somewhere between the best boy and the caterers. I can use the exposure."

"I'm a long way from sure I'll get the chance. My possible source is lying on a slab downtown."

"I heard about that. This ain't your first rodeo, Professor. You always fall into a pile of chopped liver and come up holding a twelve-buck-a-pound brisket."

AFTER HIS VISITOR left, Valentino hefted the bundle of material. Thick as it was, it was surprisingly light; the caterpillars that had produced that variety of silk were probably extinct, and the craftsmen who wove and dyed it for human consumption long in their graves, having taken with them the secrets of their trade.

Strictly speaking, the shawl's value was negligible. Without a letter of provenance, the world had only a known huckster's word that it had ever draped the shoulders of the screen's first and greatest vamp; but so far as Valentino knew, Henry had never lied to him, or even exaggerated the truth. In his way he was a man of unassailable integrity, at least when he wasn't trying to sell something. Whatever whoppers he employed in marketing the university's merchandise, they were tools only, as honorable as a surgeon's scalpel, a cabinetmaker's lathe, a master chef's carving knives; and he manipulated them with equal skill. Valentino was prepared to accept his word for anything in person, while maintaining a healthy skepticism in regard to his publicity machine. Say what you like about Henry, he never fell for his own con. Hollywood teemed with scoundrels who couldn't make that claim.

One of the few movie props still in the archivist's possession was an olive-green safe encrusted with a scrambled-egg trim of "gold leaf" (actually lead-based paint, tarnished, peeling, and undeniably toxic), a fixture in at least a dozen B-grade heist films shot on the cheap by house directors hoping to siphon off some of *The Asphalt Jungle*'s success; Charles McGraw, Mike Mazurki, and a bevy of lesser cinema yeggs had cracked it at one time or another for the entertainment of bottom-bill audiences. He rarely used it, and then only to store something of doubtful value against theft, seldom overnight. The climate-controlled safe in the laboratory the technicians used to store one-of-a-kind films was far more reliable than a primitive stage property one could ostensibly open with a smack of the hand. He rewrapped the shawl in the blue cloth, shut it inside, and spun the dial. It wobbled more than previously, and would probably one day come off in his hand.

At that moment he felt warm affection for Henry. His gesture was awfully sweet. Even if it turned out he'd mistaken a rag from a slop chest in his closet for a gift from "Auntie Theo," the thought behind it was genuine.

The archivist found Broadhead's office door open as usual;

the department head claimed to have misplaced the key long before he'd secured tenure. In sharp contrast to the office across the hall, the room was furnished as sparsely as a monk's cell, without so much as a stray paperclip to clutter it up. Its occupant sat tilted back in his deck chair, one leg slung over the other, adding exhaust from his pipe to the unhealthy air of Southern California. This violation of both state law and campus regulations represented an unspoken perk of his status as a pillar of the institution; the authorities disapproved, but kept their silence in view of the donations to the treasury he wheedled out of wealthy alumni. He'd established his academic reputation on the success of *The Persistence of Vision*, a scholarly treatise on the history and psychology of film, and now that he was at work on a sequel, those threats of forced retirement by the board of regents were bootless, and they knew it.

He wore his working uniform: a ratty cable-knit sweater, its original color buried under layers of gray ash, a polo shirt with a scientifically correct bookworm embroidered above the pocket, baggy khaki slacks, and Hush Puppies worn down almost to the soles.

"You may think I'm in deep contemplation," he said, nodding toward the venerable computer sitting idle on his desk. "I'm loafing. When I heard Ruth shrieking at that little cuttlefish from the boiler room, I nearly shut my door, just to see if the hinges still worked. What's he peddling now, Disneyland?"

Valentino told him about the gift and the story behind it.

"I'm surprised he didn't tell you he caddied for Mussolini."

"I believe him. What reason would he have to make up a story like that?"

"Depends on what he wants in return."

He felt himself grinning. "What does anyone, in this town? Screen credit."

"It's a shame the gift didn't come with a certificate of authenticity. Still, you might be able to palm it off on a fanatic, like those schmoes who keep buying the gun Wyatt Earp carried into the O.K. Corral. If Custer had had that big an arsenal, he'd have whipped Sitting Bull."

"I wouldn't think of selling it. How often does Henry give up anything for free?" A gloomy cloud scudded across his brain. "You don't suppose he's cleaning house for another reason, do you? He didn't look well."

"Henry? He'll never die. The polyester industry would never permit it. As it happens, I know his whole neighborhood's up for demolition. The regents okayed an annexation attempt there only to find out the Department of Transportation beat them to it; so our beloved Bruins won't get a new stadium with VIP boxes to fleece the fat-cat aging frat boys out of an endowment." His pipe began to make bubbling noises when he drew on it. He laid it aside to smolder out and put his feet on the floor. "How goes the Case of the White Russian's Daughter? Any luck with our stargazers?"

"Apart from knowing the difference between a pulsar and a parallax, I'm no less ignorant than I was at the start." He worried at his lower lip. "I'm considering taking Teddie Goodman up on her offer."

"She'll drop her teeth."

"That would be purely a collateral benefit. She knows where to find Carla Schmeisser, if that picture she gave me means anything. It might lead to the identity of his blackmailer, which would discharge my obligation to him and to Dinky Schwartz, if Leo comes through on his promise to fund the Comet. And with Supernova's resources behind us, we might snare *Cleopatra* after all. Jasper Grote wouldn't be the first leech who took his pay in lead instead of silver. It was Leo's good luck that one of Grote's other victims caught up with him; that's my hunch, anyway. He's no longer a threat, and I can get out of the way of the police while they track down his killer."

"Neat."

Valentino hesitated. "You only use that word when it isn't."

"No, your theory is quite tidy. I especially liked your introducing a phantom 'other' blackmail victim. It disposes of the possibility that Grote had only one, and we know who he is. He's the line the police will take, once you expand the story you told them to include him. When they've got a rat in their jaws they don't go looking for substitutes."

"Kalishnikov's no killer."

"The police in Omaha didn't agree, when he lived there. Just because they changed their mind doesn't mean the police here will go along. Knowing our Sergeant Clifford, my advice is to skedaddle down to HQ with a new statement before she finds out you forgot to mention their likely chief suspect and comes looking for you. Cops are like doctors: They don't like to make house calls."

His intercom buzzed. He flipped the switch. "Dear Ruth, what can I do for you?"

But sarcasm was lost on this receptionist; might as well try to bounce a tennis ball off a wall smeared with pitch.

"Your visitor has a visitor," came the scratchy reply. "She says she's with the police."

He switched off and frowned at Valentino. "My counsel is always sound," he said. "My timing? Not so much."

26

WHETHER SHE WAS fasting or not, Ruth's eyes—rough-cut diamonds behind her indestructible glasses—were her principal means of communication. Seated equidistant from her desk and computer, poised to pounce upon either, she flicked them in the direction of Valentino's door. Her heavily lacquered face was illegible under the best of circumstances, but the archivist thought he detected a ghost of satisfaction. It was no secret that she considered film preservation a waste of university funds and that she'd waited years for the authorities to catch on and bring the rascals to justice.

Sergeant Clifford greeted him from behind his desk. Today she wore her auburn hair clipped behind her ears, but as always this attempt at androgyny, like the mannish cut of her suit, fell short of its aim. Strangers who assumed she was a professional model learned abruptly not to repeat their mistake. Her presence alone lent his ramshackle office arrangement an air of efficiency. She carried with her the frigid logic of a glacier, as well as its inexorable progress.

"You can read into this anything you like." Her tone was

bright. "Admiral Peary, planting his flag at the North Pole and claiming it for himself. Nuts. I've been standing all day, and there's no other place to sit."

"Excuse the mess, Sergeant. If I knew you were dropping by, I'd have spruced up."

"Don't apologize. I prefer to observe my fellow creatures in their natural state. I'm like Jane Goodall that way. Gosh, you'd think I'd been watching the Discovery Channel."

Now that she'd said it, he felt even more keenly like a primitive thing under scrutiny by a superior intelligence.

"I was surprised you went to the movies with Teddie Goodman," she said. "Last I knew, you two got along like Bugs and Daffy."

He started to reply, but she held up a palm.

"The ticket clerk in that mausoleum has a gift for description. Contrary to our ditzy reputation, there are only so many women in Greater Los Angeles who look like the Dragon Lady and dress like a transvestite; fewer still who care a snap about silent films. Of course I had a head start, knowing something about you and the circle you travel in.

"But it wasn't your dating choice that made me curious. I wondered why I had to go all the way down to East L.A. to get that piece of the puzzle, after I gave you so many opportunities to bring it up last time we sat around chewing the fat."

"Did you talk to Teddie?"

"*I* talked; she never moved her lips all the time Mark David Turkus' lawyers were quoting Thomas Jefferson. I wanted to ask them to drink a glass of water, the act was that good. Anyway the gist of the conversation was we're going to need an indulgence from the Vatican just to get her to say, 'Hi, how are ya?' Well, we'll get that, we always do, but meanwhile we don't sit around playing pinochle online. So, in the interest of our past association, yours and mine, and our long-standing awareness of each other's existence, I came here."

He had jelly behind his knees. He took hold of a plastic chair heaped with lobby cards and old publicity stills, dumped them to the floor without ceremony, and sank down onto it.

"It wasn't arranged," he said, "and it certainly wasn't a date. She just showed up. I didn't think it was worth mentioning. It never occurred to me you might suspect her of murder."

"Anyone who goes around looking like that is a suspect just waiting for a crime to be charged with. When I decide I need help separating what counts in a homicide investigation from what doesn't, I'll ask the chief to put you in a cubicle downtown. It isn't fair to ask you to go on doing these things pro bono."

She glanced at the watch strapped to her wrist, a man's model in a gray metal case. She looked up, all smiles, and he felt his blood drain to his feet.

"Let's turn back the clock," she said. "We're thirty-six hours younger. Life never gives you a second chance like this, but Mama Clifford does. And, go!" She flipped open a steno pad, the narrow kind that fits in a pocket like a mushroom hunter's guide, and sat poised with the point of her mechanical pencil touching the page.

He dispensed with Teddie quickly and truthfully—if omitting yet another key piece of information fell under the category of truth. Teddie's offer to share *Cleopatra* with Supernova was plausible, provided the listener wasn't abreast of all the details of their history, and sounded kosher, he thought, without the complication of the photo of Leo Kalishnikov's daughter. As he had with the Broadheads, Valentino sketched out the scandal that had driven the theater designer west, eliminating the fact of his manufactured Russian heritage. This gave the sergeant new information: extortion as Grote's possible motive for associating himself with Kalishnikov's client, and a suggested line of investigation as to the reason for the Nebraskan's murder; Clifford's game face seemed to lift slightly at that point in his narrative.

Apart from a prick of conscience for bringing his friend into official sights, the archivist felt he hadn't betrayed any confidences. Even an old murder half a continent away was public record, and would inevitably be retrieved by any modern law-enforcement agency with or without his help, along with the former suspect's official exoneration.

Of course, an in-depth probe would also uncover his professional pose as an expatriate Russian; but it wouldn't come from Valentino.

Clifford sensed his guilt (it would be the brightest of blips on her radar), if not the full extent of its cause. She assumed a breezy bedside manner. "Look at it this way: Chiselers almost never settle for just one mark. If Grote was putting the screws to your friend, he had others on the hook. The sooner we talk to Kalishnikov, the sooner we can start whittling down the suspects."

"You're right, of course. I was in shock."

"I should think by now you'd be used to stumbling over the occasional stiff; but then no two are alike, are they? Like snowflakes—and fingerprints." She looked down at what she'd written, then back at him with a cynical kind of sympathy in her expression.

"You can say good-bye to Cleopatra and all her works. The movie was a ploy for Grote to get you involved and apply pressure from both sides with Kalishnikov in the middle. Make him squirm. That's part of the thrill for these characters, almost as much as the money; for us, too, when we nail them."

"I knew it was something like that. I guess I've known it for some time. I just didn't want to believe it." He abandoned that glum subject. "Have you made any progress?"

She was absorbed in her notes. With her head down, pencil scratching, she might have been a psychiatrist, recording every detail of their session while deciding whether to commit him.

"We recovered the murder weapon," she said without looking up: "One of those big frontier models popular with western lawmen who suckled on *Gunsmoke*. We're tracking down the registration through Washington, but right now it looks like Grote got himself disarmed, and subsequently dead. A struggle in close quarters would be consistent with the powder burns on his chest. Our killer dumped the piece in a puddle, the only one for acres. Anybody who watches TV knows what that does to fingerprints."

She looked at him then, tapping the pad with the eraser end of her pencil. Valentino noticed, abstractly, that it showed no sign of ever having been used. "That's my contribution. How about you, Mr. Film Detective? Not leaving anything else out, are we? Any other Easter eggs? Last chance."

"Sergeant, I can't think of a single thing."

SHE'D BEEN GONE less than a minute when his landline rang. The button to the interoffice line was lit. He picked up the receiver and filled Broadhead in on the conversation.

The professor cleared his throat, and he knew a dissertation was coming.

"I hate to agree with the big red dog, but she has the gift of pragmatism, scarce to find in our little part of the universe. Grote was telling some of the truth at least, about his grandfather and the Roxy Theater. That's how the film can came into the house, like pens and staplers filched from the office. It gave Grote the idea to approach Kalishnikov through you, and the means with which to do it. I suppose all those appearances you and the mad Russian have made in the human-interest columns managed to penetrate even the walls of the Corn Palace. The rest, on our down-home grifter's part, was homework: *Top Ten Lost Films: A Checklist*. That tornado in 'twenty wasn't such an ill wind where he was concerned."

"I wish I could be sure. One way or the other."

Tobacco smoke gushed near the mouthpiece in a heavy sigh. "I'm sorry, Val. The story he told you was as empty as the can. Those fabled two reels are as dead as the Sahara."

Those words were still ringing in the archivist's ears when he left work hours later; although they didn't ring so much as fall with a thud.

Disappointment was part of his job: A promising lead sputtered out, the owner of rights to a hot property stubbornly refused to surrender them or demanded a purchase price beyond the department's ability to pay, the skinflints in Accounting refused to allocate the funds necessary to secure a prize even at a bargain. The failures outnumbered the successes ten to one— which at least had the virtue of making the occasional triumph all the sweeter. But anyone with pride in his profession, and particularly an enthusiast like Valentino, took each bitter blow directly on the chin.

He was walking toward the staff parking lot, staring down at the sidewalk, when he almost collided with someone striding in the opposite direction.

"Mr. Valentino?"

The stocky young man wore the uniform of the United States Postal Service. He was the regular on that route, and Valentino recognized him, without calling his name to mind.

"Glad I caught you," the postman said. "I'm running late today. They're shooting a movie on Santa Monica. You'd think once in a while they'd stick up their barricades on somebody else's route." He thrust out a bulky package in a Mylar mailer.

Valentino had forgotten all about the parcel Ruth had told

him to expect. He was getting absent-minded about simple things like packages; what next? It was only a matter of time before he lost track of his lies and blundered his way into a cell. He accepted the item automatically, thanked the carrier, and stared at the plain label with his name and office address anonymously block-printed in black Sharpie.

Blood roared in his head, dizzying him to the point of intoxication. He felt almost sick to his stomach, as if he'd won the lottery but couldn't bring himself to believe it.

He'd handled enough similar packages to guess what they contained by their shape and weight. In more than a hundred years, and despite technical changes in the basic material, two reels of film felt basically the same.

27

THE PARCEL WAS postal service–issue, mailed two days ago from downtown. There was no return address. Fingerprints might identify the sender within hours; but that would mean turning it over to the police, and months spent in the effort to wrest it from custody while it languished in substandard conditions. Once again, in the interests of history, Valentino found himself on the wrong side of justice.

In the relative security of his car he zipped open the mailer, set it on the passenger's seat, and slid another package from inside. It was the work of a moment to remove the plastic netting, and there on his lap were two square shallow black containers, each the size of a pizza box, lightweight and of recent manufacture, secured with nylon straps and plastic buckles. The one on top bore a plain black-and-white label, produced on a modern printer:

FOX FILM
17/456

0001

This identified the year (1917) and the reel number (0001). Supposedly, it belonged to the 456th feature produced by the studio that year. Although that last figure had been misplaced, along with the movie itself, for more than a century, the October 1917 release date and the prodigious Fox output in that period made Valentino catch his breath.

He lifted away the top case just long enough to confirm that the one beneath was labeled similarly, except for the reel number: 0002. His fingers itched to undo the straps and examine what lay inside; but encouraged as he was by the careful packaging, he couldn't risk exposing the volatile material to the overheated air inside an automobile. He rewrapped the cases and poked them back into the heavy-duty envelope.

He started to call Harriet, then remembered that she'd worked the midnight shift and would be asleep after winding down at home for a few hours. There was no one else in existence—not even Kyle Broadhead—with whom he was prepared to share this discovery at this moment.

And there was still the possibility—assuming these were indeed reels of film—that they were part of a cruel and elaborate hoax—blank frames possibly, or some clumsy amateur production—intended to humiliate him at an unveiling before witnesses. That would be Jasper Grote's last jest.

Valentino's own department offered the ideal screening facilities, but there were too many prying eyes, and entirely too much shared interest in the subject; privacy was the first casualty of academic fervor.

He started the car and headed toward The Oracle.

The landmark billboard on Sunset was advertising a new feature: *Murder, She Wrote: The Motion Picture*. The gimlet eyes of Cate Blanchett, starring as Jessica Fletcher, seemed to follow him all the way down the block.

This reminded him of Teddie and her army of spies. He

turned off the boulevard and took evasive measures. The thousands of hours he'd logged in front of detective movies, and familiarity with his adopted city, led him down byways and alleys and through parking lots, checking his mirrors for suspicious vehicles, until he was reasonably certain he'd thrown off any surveillance.

Just in case someone was watching the theater, he drove around the building, parked in the deep shade of the carport he'd had built onto the back, and carried the package to the fire exit, using his body to conceal his burden from the neighboring office building. As required by the fire code, the steel door opened from inside without hindrance, but could be entered from the alley only after punching a complicated series of numbers and letters into a keypad; the sequence meant nothing to anyone but himself. Taking all these precautions made him feel like a cross between James Bond and a class-A paranoid; but as Kyle had told him more than once, people with persecution complexes tended to die peacefully in bed.

His hope, that the contract workers he'd hired—true to the creed of the profession—had disappeared for the day, evaporated when he let himself into the plain rear entryway and heard the whine of a power saw upstairs. Fine plaster dust, impossible to contain regardless of the precautions taken, drifted down the homely back stairs like powdery snow. He mounted to the mezzanine, located the foreman in his hard hat, safety glasses, and breathing mask, and shouted his request above the din. The man leaned in to hear. He nodded, rolling his eyes (there was no explaining the whims of a property owner!), and signaled to his crew to stop and pack up.

Years of writing checks had resigned Valentino to the increased cost of labor caused by yet another delay; but in any case the Queen of the Nile was worth the sacrifice.

He waited impatiently while tools were packed away and

safety features reinstalled, locked the front door behind the last straggler, and retired to his apartment/projection room. There he cleared space to work amid the rubble (the project appeared no closer to completion than it had for months) and sat down in the leather recliner—a gift from his friends in the department upon the completion of original construction, comfortable to rest in between reel changes or simply to watch a movie without interruption—and undid the fastenings on the box marked 0001.

He put on cotton gloves and lifted out a round flat receptacle of synthetic material, a technical improvement over corrosive metal. His heart thumped in his throat as he pried off the lid.

It was clean inside and out. He sniffed and detected no sharp stench of vinegar. Any chemical deterioration that might have occurred since the original storage appeared to have been arrested. He inspected the glossy black stuff wound around a reel of modern manufacture, non-corrosive also and free of irregularities that might damage the fragile sprocket holes. Folded Tyvek packets were arranged around the reel; they resembled common balloon wrap, but were far more sophisticated. Slimy character though he was, Grote had taken care to protect his merchandise—but then Valentino had no solid evidence that the parcel had come by way of the Nebraskan.

Still, he'd hinted at an expert connection, and had demonstrated an amateur understanding of the steps required in order to preserve volatile celluloid stock. The evidence in favor of his story was piling up, even if his motives were doubtful.

Valentino unspooled two feet of film and held it up to the light. When the title card appeared, he almost dropped the reel in a nervous spasm. With both hands he rewound the footage and returned the reel to its container. He was hyperventilating. He sat absolutely still with his hands resting on his thighs until his respiration returned to normal.

He inspected the more reliable of his two projectors, opening all the compartments, removing dust with a specially treated cloth, applying drops of light oil to the gears and wiping away the excess. Finally he changed gloves, fitted Reel One onto the machine, threaded the blank leader through the gate and around the pickup wheel at the bottom; whispering as he did so the arcane names of the various parts: Upper steady feed sprocket, upper feed film floor, fire shutter, intermittent sprocket, lower feed film loop, lower steady feed sprocket, etc.; a sort of jump-rope rhyme, ingrained in him since film school, and as automatic as breathing.

He swung the reel into place with a satisfying *chunk*, took a deep breath, and flipped the switch.

The motor purred and a shaft of white light shot through the square opening before him, across the auditorium, and splashed onto the screen. And then he sat back to watch.

28

THE EXISTING FOOTAGE made one thirst for more.

There was a sea battle in the Mediterranean, hand-to-hand combat on land with swords and maces, the burning of the Roman galleys, the destruction of the great library at Alexandria, Cleopatra tumbling out of a rolled rug at Caesar's feet, her spectacular entry into Rome (elephants, camels, Nubian warriors, vestal virgins, and all), their cynical romance, and then—nothing. It ended with the conqueror's death in the Roman forum, with so much drama left to the imagination, a play without a third act.

The assassination was balletic: Horrific poetry in motion, beautifully filmed. The scenes of carnage on land and at sea unfolded in montage, surprisingly sophisticated for such an experimental technique. The triumphal parade through the gates of the Eternal City was Byzantine, barbaric, and splendid enough to have inspired Cecil B. DeMille—then honing his craft along more modest proportions at his snake-infested ranch in the Valley—to fill the early screen with over-the-top ornamentation. Fox's pursuit of technical perfection bordered on monomania.

Plot wise, the rest—the part of the film that was missing—was predictable. Wily as Caesar's lover was, as cavalier as Hollywood could be when it came to fact and legend, the story could only end as fate, history, and drama had ordained. Yet Valentino felt cheated. The savage passion of the love affair with Marc Antony, the bloodshed at Actium, the double-suicide at the close; lost. Valentino had been abandoned on the edge of a cliff.

It sent him all the way back to Indiana, when the film broke in the last reel of *The Three Musketeers* just as D'Artagnan was getting the worst of it in a swordfight, and the audience was sent home by the manager of the neighborhood theater with an apology and a refund. The boy wandered away in a fog of unfulfilled expectation. It was one of those miserable memories of childhood that lingered.

Cleopatra's flaws—for it was a product of its time, and more a period piece than an enduring classic—were immaterial. He was familiar enough with an art form in its nascency to disregard the hyper-theatrical physical gestures (some critics likened them to a windmill in a hurricane) and settle quickly into the rhythm of a time that had become as remote to contemporary America as Cleopatra's Egypt must have seemed to jazz-age audiences.

For this viewer, the outdated nature of the film was the essence of its charm. He found himself admiring the plaster-of-paris columns and painted muslin lintels just as if they were genuine marble; and he asked himself, *Who's to say the eunuchs and sentinels of the ancient world didn't arch their brows and swing their arms just this way?* The screen was twenty feet wide after all, and must be filled.

And really, was Theda's fish-eyed stare any more ludicrous than Elizabeth Taylor's broad, burlesque wink in the 1963 remake, aimed at Rex Harrison from atop a parade float shaped like the Sphinx? It turned the blare of the stereophonic trumpets into a raspberry. Primitive as the silent feature must appear to an audience unschooled in Life Before Facebook, it was the raw nature of this unpolished gem that appealed to the archivist.

On the eve of America's entry into World War One, the motion picture was less than twenty years old. It was making itself up as it went along, would not be an industry for a decade; and unlike any other art form, it lurched toward perfection in real time and in full view of the world. You saw it take its first uncertain steps, find its balance, and break into a run, all at first hand.

And there were the leading lady's costumes! Fifty, if the press kits in his collection didn't exaggerate, and close to that many in this fragment: dripping with rubies and diamonds, trimmed with peacock feathers and golden snakes, made from gossamer and real leopard skins (PETA would surely picket the premiere), each ensemble more outrageous than the last. Her wardrobe on that one feature would have sustained Mae West throughout her career. Nothing in that gaudy era succeeded quite like excess.

To experience it here, in a plaster palace where the star herself would feel at home, was to appreciate her in her natural element. Could she act? Unimportant. Even without a live orchestra to accompany her (as it would upon release), her presence carried the film.

She was a pioneer: Webster's dictionary had coined the word *vamp* for her exclusively. She was "It" when Clara Bow was in pinafores, a sex symbol a generation ahead of Jean Harlow, a bombshell before Marilyn Monroe was born. Whether they knew it or not, female leads as late as Julia Roberts and Catherine Zeta-Jones had assembled themselves from parts left over from Theda Bara.

The tailpiece flapped through the gate, the screen went blank. But phantom images lingered, like a dream in the half-world of awakening.

"Shame about those missing last reels," said a voice at his back. "They say Bill Fox had a genuine asp flown in all the way from Egypt. It'd be interesting to see how it measures up against animatronics."

The voice—as would *any* voice, after forty minutes of silence broken only by the clicking of the frames passing through the gate—brought Valentino to his feet, his heart galloping; the husky tones of the woman who'd entered the room without making a sound nearly pitched him over into the auditorium a full story below.

He turned. Silhouetted in the empty doorway, dressed unconventionally as always, in a form-fitting sheath that seemed to shift and change colors in the light reflecting from the empty screen, Teddie and Theodosia Burr Goodman became one, a miracle of double-exposure.

Movie magic? Tell the truth and call it black magic.

HE SWITCHED OFF the projector. That deflected the light, carving deep and disturbing shadows beneath her prominent cheekbones, the fathomless sockets of her magnificent eyes. He saw the skull beneath the flesh.

Which was hardly necessary. The image of Teddie Goodman standing here, in his most private place on earth, was like something from a weird fantasy comic book: *The Ghoul's Revenge.*

She'd visited only once before, to end up in a broken heap at the bottom of the stairs to the projection room. Her attempt to burglarize the place had backfired, thanks to someone even more ruthless than she. But months of medical treatment and physical therapy had failed to inspire a change in her ways.

"I'm beginning to think you really are a vampire," he said, when he'd recovered his composure. "You can turn yourself into vapor and drift in through a keyhole."

Excellent teeth assumed the shape—if not the reality—of a smile. It made her look more skeletal still.

"I hate disappointing people, especially when they pay me a compliment; but I was already in the building when you were bumping around like a pinball, turning latches and twisting keys. I knew there was only one place you'd go once you had that package in your hands."

He was no match for her when it came to subterfuge. Try what he would, throw off every tail, secure every lock; the flaw in his character would betray him inevitably. He couldn't be on the alert all the time; it wasn't in him. Sooner or later he must relax his guard, and she'd be right there to take advantage of it.

He'd almost run into that postman, he'd been that preoccupied. The die was cast before he made his first cautious move. She'd told him all about her private detectives—knowing he'd forget all about them just when it counted most.

"Does Turkus know how you use your expense account?"

"Legitimate business deductions. I didn't earn a parking space next to the boss's by saving him pennies."

"Write this one off as a loss. No charge for the sneak preview, Teddie. If you want to know what happened before you came in, you can buy a ticket to the premiere like everyone else."

She wore a sleek fur draped over one shoulder, which she let slide onto the back of his chair; it was like a snake shedding its skin.

"Don't crow," she said; "it doesn't suit you. To possess isn't to own. Unless, of course, that package came with a document giving you the legal right to show the film in public. If not, you need our organization to track down the holder, and our stable of attorneys to swing a deal."

"We've done it before. It just takes us a little longer. The world's waited more than a century for *Cleopatra*. What's a couple of years more?"

"A couple of years in a properly controlled environment isn't the same as a couple of years in a stuffy police property room. You know as well as I do that silver nitrate's less stable than green bananas."

He managed a semblance of laughter.

"Squeal to the police? You? Is there no honor among thieves?"

"It's the duty of every citizen to come forward with evidence in a criminal investigation."

He felt himself grow pale. How much did she know?

"You're bluffing," he said. "You wouldn't risk destroying a prize like *Cleopatra* just to teach me a lesson."

"You know my record: I'm an acquisitions professional, not a cinema buff. The whole of silent cinema could go up in a puff of smoke and it wouldn't affect my appetite, only my bank account; which can be replaced. There's always another pot of gold at the base of some rainbow. Go ahead; call my bluff."

It was a Mexican standoff, and he wasn't fluent in the language. He'd been wrong to face her across her own poker table. He shifted his weight from one foot to the other, buying time.

Something crackled in his inside breast pocket.

He'd forgotten it was there.

"I do know you," he said then. "You only use the scorched-earth policy when you're fresh out of alternatives. You're forgetting you still have a card to play; one that won't involve destroying a property we both want.

"Now's the time to play it, Teddie. Put up or shut up."

29

"IS THERE A neutral place where we can discuss this further?" Teddie asked after a few minutes. "Here in this boneyard I'm outnumbered ten to one by what's left of all your dead friends."

Valentino suppressed a smile, lest she notice and suspect an ambush. Just to have made this human juggernaut stop and think in mid-charge was a sign of hope. "I know just the place."

She waited while he rewound the reels, and watched with frank interest as he slid them in their state-of-the-art containers into a steel cabinet and locked it. Although he and she were under a kind of truce and the property was safe for the time being (say what one would about Teddie, she behaved herself as long as there was a chance of getting what she was after without the bother of a scheme), Valentino knew she was storing the information for future reference. He made a mental note to arrange more secure storage before their next round of hostilities—and to call a contractor and add a professional guard to his bill. In all likelihood she could pick the lock with a sharp look. It wouldn't be the first time she'd stooped to burglary, and in this very place.

People without scruples often assume the affliction is universal. She refused to ride in his car, and he—*knowing* she couldn't be relied upon—was reluctant to trust her behind the wheel with him as a passenger. In her world, speed limits and one-way streets were only suggestions; she was capable of playing chicken with rush-hour traffic just to frighten him into signing off on a one-sided deal. At length they agreed to drive separately.

He couldn't resist saying it:

"You shouldn't need directions. I'm pretty sure you know where that picture was taken."

She paused in the midst of arranging her fur over her shoulders, cape-fashion, to give him a look of cool appraisal. "You figured it out; congratulations. You must have had help."

"I've lived here all my adult life," was all he said in response. It had taken Kyle Broadhead to point it out to him; but he'd be hanged rather than give her the satisfaction of a confession.

She turned up her collar, as if she were chilled: She was a cold-blooded creature after all. "What are we waiting for? To infinity—and beyond."

Mockery came naturally to her; but in this case, he knew, it wasn't just to cause annoyance. It was to remind him who was holding the trump card. He had the film, but she had Carla Schmeisser, *née* Kalishnikov.

SHE DROVE A Tesla; anything less conspicuous would have disappointed him. It was as long as a lifeboat and built so low it barely showed in his rearview mirror. The finish, like its owner's outfit, changed shades with each alteration in the cloud cover; once again he thought of a snake's skin. It was the perfect get-away car for a bank job: No two eyewitnesses would agree on the color. He could barely keep his eyes off it all the way up the Hollywood Hills.

Griffith Park had leapt to his mind the instant she'd proposed a meeting on common ground. The observatory was a
smudge in the background of the picture Teddie had given him
back at the Priest's Hole—a thousand years ago, it seemed. It
had pleased him on a subconscious level to turn that tease into
a possible solution to their differences; but if Supernova's super-
sleuth was affected by this irony, the fact was no more apparent
than the hum of the electric motor pulling her along behind
him.

He redirected his gaze from the mirror and the pavement
ahead to consider the scenery, the tall firs outside the windows. Somewhere among them, Leo Kalishnikov's daughter
had paused briefly in her journey from the American Heartland
to wicked L.A. to pose for an unknown photographer (Teddie
herself, perhaps? Just how far into the conspiracy did she figure?). The apparent age of the woman in the shot corresponded
roughly with her date of birth. The session might have been
as recent as a month—or five years, depending on the rate at
which one aged physically. In any case, how the snapshot had
found its way into Teddie's hands was less important than how
she'd arrived at the familial connection, and just what it had
to do with *Cleopatra*—and, of course, Jasper Grote's murder.
He had to keep reminding himself that that was the feature of
interest to the authorities.

"Jasper, Jasper," he murmured. "Who killed you and why?
Because you were a blackmailer, or to get your hands on a rare
and valuable piece of motion-picture history, or for some other
reason? It wasn't your endearing personality, to that I can swear.

"And was it you who sent me *Cleopatra*? And if so, why?
Whether you hoped to sell it to the university for a price ten
times what it cost to produce it, or you were just using it as a
trick to put your extortion victim in the middle, the logical approach was the same: A bargaining chip is useless unless you

withhold it. Handing it over in the middle of negotiations—if indeed it was you, Grote, who sent it, as one of your last acts—made absolutely no sense."

They turned into the park. At that hour on a weekday the paths belonged to silver-haired retirees, dogs on leashes, and walkers on wheels. Ahead, the triple domes of the observatory gleamed like polished porcelain against a sky uncharacteristically clear of smut. The Tesla whispered into a space next to his and they walked up to the building; but instead of going inside he led her around to the side, where they looked down on the back of the Hollywood sign, the best-known landmark this side of the Eiffel Tower, perched on the hillside; but from this angle they couldn't see it from its intended angle, only raw wood where the paint had flecked off. It was like looking out from inside a mirror; La-La Land stripped of its fairy-tale wonder.

"Legend has it all the sets from the silent *Ben-Hur* are buried among these hills. Some of the young buffs come up here with metal detectors, searching for Roman helmets and gold-plated goblets."

He pointed down at the basin at their feet. There was only a light haze today. "I've been here when it's so thick down there you can only see the tops of a few skyscrapers, the Watts Towers. It's like the ruins of a lost civilization. *The Planet of the Apes*: You know, the Statue of Liberty—"

He realized she was staring at him.

"My God," she said. "You take all your lady friends up here, don't you, give them that same speech? It's a wonder you ever get laid."

He'd been about to say that it was on this spot where James Dean had squared off with a juvenile delinquent, wielding a switchblade in *Rebel Without a Cause*. He'd forgotten his audience.

She'd as much as told him she knew what had prompted

him to select this site for their meeting. Not that it affected her nerves. She could stand before the Inquisition, with the evidence of her heresy in plain sight on the judges' bench, and not flick an eyelash.

He got right to it.

"I chose this place because we could be alone at this hour, and because it was on my mind; as of course you know."

He breathed in and out. "I can't promise anything, Teddie. Whether we can go partners with Supernova on the release of *Cleopatra* is up to the administration. Someone will want to know why we're even negotiating, with the film already in UCLA's possession. Smith Oldfield in Legal knows as much as your team about copyright law—assuming *anyone* holds the rights. I'm just guessing, but it seems to me that after more than a century the property's probably in public domain."

"Then why drag me up here at all? I've seen the Milky Way, and it's got nothing on the Ginza Strip. You'll remember I snagged *Seven Samurai* out from under you on that trip."

"Sixty-seven minutes of it, you mean."

"Every minute of which no one had seen for forty years. Stick to the subject."

"You know what I want." He slid the photo from his inside pocket and held it up.

She didn't even look at it. "So I'm supposed to give you Leo Kalishnikov's little Russian dumpling in return for 'I can't promise anything, Teddie'? Lord, you're pathetic! To think I'd fall into a swoon just because of the scenery." She took a step toward the parking lot.

Instinctively he put a hand on her bare forearm. The skin was as smooth as oil.

"You're forgetting there's a murder involved. You know as well as I do you're not out of the woods just because Sergeant Clifford let you go when Turkus' lawyers stonewalled her. She'll come back at you with a court order, and if you clam up this time she'll jail you as a material witness. I've been there, don't forget. It isn't fun. How many times do you think the Turk will bail you out before he decides the game isn't worth the price of the candle?"

Her smile might have been painted on a wall for all the warmth it contained. She took his wrist between thumb and forefinger, lifted it away from hers, and let it drop.

"One reason I never watch the films I bag is I won't be seduced; as if I could. Take the advice of a pro: You shouldn't try to imitate what you see. It takes stones to read a movie cop's lines and make them stick. If the skinflints you work for would spend a buck on your department instead of the athletics program, you'd have access to a database that would match everyone on earth to her biological roots; but that'll never happen, just as you'll always play second-unit to me because you've got popcorn for brains."

"What else do you want?"

"What you can't give. If you think I'm after *Cleopatra* just for the credit of taking an elephant, you don't know me. You were born with an edge: The only thing you've got in common with Rudolph Valentino is the name—a name that wasn't even his, by the way; but still it's your key to every door in this cheap town. I don't have that, even though I'm entitled to it by blood and you're not."

She straightened to her full height: In her mind, she was six feet tall in her stocking feet. Her nostrils flared and her pale polished cheeks stained the shade of red she usually reserved for her lips. At that moment she was a dead ringer for her namesake.

"Maybe if I corner the market on Theda Bara," she said, "scrape up every surviving frame of film she appeared in and get my name in the restoration credits, the world will associate me with her, at least by proxy, and the playing field will be even. I wouldn't need Supernova's resources or this ludicrous masquerade." She raised both hands and swept them to the ground, taking herself in from head to foot. "Don't you think I know people are laughing behind me when I prance around dressed and made up like a cartoon vamp? But they don't forget me, and they recognize me next time. Once I've established my brand I can throw away that crutch; build on my reputation and no one else's, in a baseball cap and jeans with the knees ripped out. Can you give me that, and still hog *Cleopatra*? Thought not."

Her heels clicked on the pavement, followed by the bang of the Tesla's door and the sibilant whisper of the engine coming to life.

30

VALENTINO SAID, "SHE'S delusional."

For Harriet, he'd finally come through with all the details of his latest adventure, from Leo Kalishnikov's personal and professional predicaments to his potential involvement in Dinky Schwartz's drive-in theater scheme—if Valentino managed to identify the theater designer's blackmailer—to the inexplicable appearance of the missing film reels and finally his conversations with Teddie in The Oracle and at the Griffith Observatory. It was all so complicated he'd had to keep going back to fill in gaps he'd left in the narrative. Harriet had listened without interrupting.

Although she was out of bed when he returned to the apartment, she was still in pajamas, a blue quilted robe, and the man's slippers she preferred on her long narrow feet ("Garbo-like," Valentino called them; "clodbusters," she insisted). She sat facing him in the breakfast nook, bobbing a tea bag up and down in her cup without drinking, just watching the water take on color. When she could no longer see the bag for the murk, it would be ready to drink.

"I never bought Leo's story," she said. "He couldn't leave it alone. One day he was the great-grandson of a grand duke; next day his Uncle Sergei played croquet with Trotsky." She lifted out the bag and examined it, as if it were at fault. She immersed it again. "I'm not so sure she *is* delusional."

"Teddie?" he said. "You weren't there. When she stood up straight and did that thing with her arms, all she needed was an organ piping in the background to channel the grand and glorious Theda. I almost went out for popcorn."

"What did you expect? Once a diva, always a diva."

"I tell you she's gotten worse. She's played that role so long she's fallen for her own publicity."

"Not an unusual affliction in this town."

"She raises it to the level of art."

"Still, have you considered the possibility she might be telling the truth?"

"Not you, too! If *you* slip your chocks, I won't have anyone to hold me down except Kyle, and you know how it grates on me when he plays Greek chorus."

She shook her head. How she managed to appear so fresh and dewy-eyed on six hours' sleep following a twelve-hour shift was one of the many mysteries that kept him interested in her.

"Think about it," she said. "You say because Teddie's crooked she thinks the whole world's on the make, but you're just as bad. You've been playing chess with her so long you *expect* her to cheat; but if you've figured it right this time, and she's got all the pieces she needs, what's she got to gain by bending the rules? She told you straight out she can link anyone in the world to an ancestor through the facilities Supernova's given her. Maybe she wasn't just talking about Carla Schmeisser and Kalishnikov."

He gave her a blank look.

She leaned forward and punched him in the chest. "It's a clue, you dummy!"

He was too caught up in what she'd said to rub the sore spot.

"It takes more than a genealogical program to prove family."

"Thanks for the lesson! Of course, us dopes in criminal forensics don't know from DNA; can't even spell it." She frowned again at her tea, took a sip, made a face, put down the cup, and went back to bobbing. "It's not *proof* I'm talking about. Before DNA, there were family trees. They established the likelihood of heredity by tracing names: Census figures, marriage records, birth certificates, family Bibles, letters and journals. Back then it was only a matter of preponderance of evidence, which science today can narrow down to a biological certainty."

"Are you saying she might be right?"

"Been saying it right along. You and Kyle have always gone on the assumption that Theodosia Goodman—our Teddie—is an invention. What if that's her real name? What if she can establish a line of succession back to Cincinnati, where Theda Bara was born, or a one-night stand in Beverly Hills, followed by a period of confinement in Havana? Wouldn't that give her at least bragging rights to her idol's legacy?"

"It wouldn't give her the authority to have Theda's remains exhumed in order to collect tissue samples—blood, hair follicles, whatever—to compare with hers; she said so herself. Since there are no known relatives to provide any, it's hopeless. Without science—"

"We've established I'm not talking about absolute proof. Until we solved the puzzle of the human genome, the process I just described swayed a lot of judges and juries in the petitioner's favor. It's still strong enough for the interested party to make the claim, whether or not she's legally entitled to the goods and chattel connected with it. With the resources she has at her command, she could force the issue before the bench; but if she fails, she hasn't a chance in hell of getting a second shot. That's why she's pushing so hard for scientific corroboration; why the ice queen lost her cool."

"If I wanted to hear lawyer talk, I'd have made an appointment with Fanta."

Harriet sipped again, sighed, and sat back, legs crossed, cradling her cup and saucer. "I'm not in court; but if I were, I'd be delivering my summation. Teddie may not be able to make her case, but based on the evidence at hand, no well-instructed jury would find her guilty of fraud."

"So what you're telling me is that in order to get her to put me in touch with Carla Schmeisser, who may or may not be able to tell me who's been blackmailing her father, and what Jasper Grote has to do with anything—which may or may not get the police off my neck—I have to prove *our* Theodosia Goodman shares her genes with *the* Theodosia Goodman."

"In a nutshell."

"I wish someone would tell me what that phrase means."

"Just because the subject's knotty doesn't mean you should change it."

He scowled at nothing, then shook his head. "I'm beginning to miss those days when all I had to do was solve a murder for the LAPD."

"Oh, you'll probably have to do that too. Why mess with the pattern?"

"Now you sound like Henry Anklemire. He's always ready to turn a plug in the police columns into a full-page ad in the entertainment section. Sometimes I—"

He almost thought she'd punched him again, it had come to him that suddenly; an echo of something he'd said himself moments ago. He shot to his feet, jarring the table and slopping tea out of her cup. He was at the hallway door before she could shake the scalding liquid from her hand; when she did, curiosity got the better of annoyance.

"I know that look," she said. "The last time I saw it, you thought you'd traced Mary Pickford's first talking picture to a landfill in Guam."

"Guadalajara." He spoke automatically. "And it was her last silent, not her first talkie. I know how to give Teddie what she wants. I've had it all day." He swung open the door.

Sergeant Lucille Clifford stood facing him with one fist raised to knock. She looked sporty in houndstooth tweeds and knee-length boots. "Maestro!" she said. "Can I interest you in a trip to my little sweatshop in West Hollywood? I can offer you Starbuck's and my mother-in-law's homemade coffee cake. Of course, if you're watching your waistline—" She opened her fist to dangle a pair of handcuffs.

31

WEST HOLLYWOOD HOMICIDE occupied a place out of time; a homely pile erected on a foundation of asbestos and quicklime, and durable to the point of fanatical obsession. It would take the Big One to dislodge it, and then the city would just rebuild it, brick by crumbling brick, in all its dispiriting detail.

The squad room might have been lifted straight out of a hundred old movies: the water cooler gulping in a corner, the curling linoleum tiles on the floor, the corkboard with its ever-increasing strata of fugitive circulars (dating back, Valentino firmly believed, to John Dillinger); but there was more to the place than just a matter of life imitating art. It was on this visit that the archivist discovered the key to its dehumanizing effect: It lacked cubicles.

All the desks stood out in the open, naked to the world, in a room that carried sound like the surface of a lake. Some of the most sensitive information in existence changed hands within earshot of a dozen people at a time, including strangers from the street. A civilian such as he—a "person of interest" in a criminal investigation—was constantly aware that all of his secrets were pouring unfiltered into the public domain.

The interview rooms down the hall were a little more private, but only insofar as a window separated the guest of honor from the curious onlooker (and the rooms were wired, as Valentino well knew). He had expected nothing else. He'd raised Sergeant Clifford's displeasure by withholding crucial information and, poet of justice that she was, she would proceed to grill him in public with his pants down.

Still, there was no limit to her power to shock.

Stepping off the elevator, she led him past a row of mismatched chairs, all of them empty except for the one where Leo Kalishnikov sat, wearing a white Palm Beach suit with a crisp Panama hat on his lap and looking very much like a convicted felon awaiting his sentence.

HE WAS ANCIENT suddenly. His age was part of the façade he turned to the world, as much as his picaresque wardrobe and the fleeting quality of his eastern European accent; now he was just a beaten old man. The skin of his neck hung loose over the knot of his necktie and the weight of it appeared to be dragging his large ears down toward his shoulders.

No word or gesture passed between them—they might have been strangers for all the recognition Kalishnikov showed—and then Valentino was following Clifford through a door into one of the glassed-in rooms.

"That man has a head made for hats," she said, waving him into one of a pair of chairs drawn up to the table. "Makes me jealous. I can't wear one but that everybody in the ranks calls me Annie Hall. Hell on discipline."

"What have you been doing to him? He looks a hundred."

"I can't take credit for a man's conscience. When we tramped the Valley with your picture and Grote's—yeah, we got one, tell you about it later—we dug up a waitress who saw you breaking bread with him. Next time she looked, you'd traded one old man for another. We'd have pegged Kalishnikov faster if that night he hadn't decided to dress like a regular human being, but she overheard some of your talk, and that comic-opera accent struck a tardy chord with me, all the way back to when you started on that theater of yours.

"So we hauled him in, and guess what? When he tried zipping his lips and we asked him about his citizenship status, he smiled! Well, you can't threaten a witness with deportation when it turns out he was born in Nebraska. When we finally got that out of him, he stopped smiling and fell apart like a row of dominoes. Some friend you are. You could've spared him some sweat."

"It wasn't my secret to tell."

"See, that's the thing about secrets." She drew out the chair opposite, sat, and rested her forearms on the table. Her man's watch caught the overhead fluorescents in a bright circle like the eye of God. "They're not like a house that comes with a deed, or a car that comes with a title. Once it involves us cops it's community property. You can't hog it without making us wonder just what else you've got poked away."

His throat worked, but he said nothing.

She leaned in and took his hands in hers. The obscene intimacy of the gesture sent a charge of cold electricity all the way to his shoulders. She smiled. "I saw you swallow just now. You *wanted* to say Kalishnikov's not the type to commit murder, but you didn't, because as the man who promised to help him out of his jam, that makes you the next likely suspect."

Out of the corner of his eye he glimpsed a face turned partway toward the window from the hallway; the sagging profile of an old man in a white suit that fit him like a shroud. And she saw him see it. She patted his hands and let go.

"I can't fool you; you've seen all the movies. He thinks I'm thanking you for coming clean and he's this close to adding a pair of bracelets to his sporty ensemble. That's a compliment. I considered parking you out there next to him, because I had you down as the weaker party. I was wrong. He's the better suspect, having been tied to one killing already, and the man with the most to lose: The man we're more likely to jump on with both feet when you've sold him out."

He felt beyond weary, beyond demoralized. He was desperately tired, as if he'd been pushing a boulder up the same hill for days. "I don't know that I have anything to add to what you've already found out."

She sat back. "We can always use something to fill in the cracks and holes. You know, spackle."

And so for the second time that day he told it all, or most of it, inserting new information into the blanks: Dinky, The Comet, his deal with Kalishnikov, Grote, the anonymous package he'd received, and Carla Schmeisser, not overlooking the picture Teddie had given him. Clifford, he knew, would draw the conclusion that she wanted to trade her for Supernova's half-interest in *Cleopatra*. He saw no reason to hang Teddie's dirty laundry—her need for a blood connection to Theda Bara—out in public.

It all came forth in so orderly a fashion, he having been through it so recently, it seemed too smooth, even to him. There was something about a police station that made the unvarnished truth sound like a lie.

But instead of jumping on him with her lady's size nines, she nodded.

"I wanted to hear it before you gussied it up for the official record. Care to guess who sent you those film reels?"

"Grote?"

"Yes and no. Yes, because no one knew *Cleopatra* was in play

brush with the law, and your professional relationship with him isn't exactly top secret.

"When we found out Grote was a pro, everything made sense. He was running a variation on the old badger game, looking to pinch Kalishnikov between him and you. You'd be so keen on getting your hands on that film, you'd agree to press him to pay off; you know, as a friend."

"Grote thought wrong if he thought that."

"It wouldn't throw him. These characters always have a plan B. If you bailed, he'd just do it the old-fashioned way and put the screws directly to Kalishnikov.

"Then again," she said, "maybe he already did."

"You think that's your killer out in the hall."

"He's a con man, same as Handy; he's just sailed inside the law till now. That kind's as smart as crooks get. He knew you'd be next in line for the rap, so why not park the corpse in your passenger seat?"

Valentino shook his head. He was surprised something didn't come loose inside and rattle.

"I'm not a detective, as you keep reminding me. I don't see a murderer behind every face. And I don't see what Leo's daughter has to do with this."

"Me neither. I was hoping you could tell me. Guess now I'll have to make another run at Teddie Goodman, see if I can crack that nut. Maybe obstruction of justice in a homicide can make Turkus shake loose of her. You know, the Hollywood power bloc isn't what it used to be. The Me-Too Movement drove a truck straight through it."

Someone rapped on the door. "Yeah?" she snapped. Scratch a cop, find a frustrated actor; she'd been robbed of her curtain line.

Korbut, the uniform, came in, leaned over her, and whispered in her ear.

She said, "Cuffs on?"

"Yes, ma'am." He sounded hurt.

She looked at Valentino. "You're off the hook, DeMille. The old man just confessed."

IV

THAT SHAWL, FOLKS!

32

SERGEANT CLIFFORD WAS in a rare good mood; which was seldom shared by anyone facing her in an interrogation room. She ordered an officer to drive him wherever he wanted in a squad car. Seated behind the man, hemmed in behind a bullet-proof shield and between locked doors without handles, the passenger delivered his decision.

"Oracle, what's that?"

It was Valentino's particular brand of luck to have drawn one of the rare citizens of Los Angeles unfamiliar with its principal culture. He gave him the address.

Alighting on the sidewalk to let him out, the officer—a William Bendix type, with a neck as big around as his head—stared at the Greco-Roman-Polynesian-Byzantine-Gothic-Moorish-Goldwynian façade, the terra-cotta moldings pinkish in the reflected glow of the settling sun, the upraised index finger of the marquee ringed by cold electric bulbs. Snap-on letters thanked patrons for their patience during renovation.

"Doesn't look like it's open."

"I live here."

"No kidding? Where do you go on a Saturday night, the library?"

His passenger put one foot on the curb and paused. A row of pickups took up all the available spaces in front of the theater and power tools shrilled through an open window upstairs; but that wasn't what had stopped him. He remembered where he'd been headed when Clifford had intercepted him at Harriet's door. His heart rate went up, and with it his spirits.

"Change of plans, Officer. Please take me to UCLA. The main campus."

"That place I know," said the other, climbing back behind the wheel. "I got my master's there."

Which was the difference between real life and Central Casting.

He found Kyle Broadhead seated at Ruth's desk, reading a computer printout with his pipe clamped between his teeth.

Valentino said, "You're not that much of an improvement over the original. I thought she was wired in here with the mainframe."

"She's at the dentist's, getting her fangs cleaned. I'm supposed to answer the phone and not stink up the place while doing it." He relit the pipe. "Speaking of which, I smell the disinfectant they use downtown. Did the Big Red Dog send her regards?"

"She's arrested Kalishnikov for Jasper Grote's murder."

"Impossible. Eccentrics don't kill people."

"He confessed."

Broadhead set aside the sheet.

"Well, it sounds more interesting than this sophomore's psychosexual interpretation of *Wrestling Women vs. the Aztec Mummy*. Just what clever scheme have you come up with to set the planet back in its orbit this time around?"

Valentino told him.

"Anklemire, now," Broadhead said. "*Him* I could buy for Grote.

That little thimble-rigger is capable of carrying on both sides of an argument and inciting himself to violence. What makes you think he wasn't selling you one of his wooden lightning-rods?"

"Can't think what he had to gain, apart from a smaller moving bill. Care to take a look?"

"Wouldn't be as much fun as this." He picked up the printout, selected one of Ruth's pencils from a cup emblazoned with the insignia of the United States Marine Corps, and drew a bold *F* on the top of the sheet. "Call me when Teddie gets you in a half-Nelson. I'll bring the Jaws of Life."

When Valentino came back out of his office carrying his bundle, Broadhead was on the phone. They exchanged waves.

So far as Valentino knew, the bungalow Teddie Goodman maintained at the Beverly Hills Hotel was strictly a place to change outfits between business liaisons; where she ate and slept was an industry secret. Nevertheless it was the only reliable address he had for this agent-without-portfolio, who had an office in the Supernova building but seldom visited it.

The desk clerk in the palatial lobby—a Latina too lovely for her job but apparently not quite breathtaking enough for a screen test—assessed him coolly and without obvious judgment, then lifted her receiver and pecked out a number. In L.A., an off-the-rack jacket and jeans shiny in the knees could as well clothe a billionaire as a beachcomber.

He could hear the line purring; the stress-inducing sound of a phone ringing without answer. The clerk was taking the receiver away from her ear when a low-pitched voice came on.

"A Mr. Valentino to see you, Miss Goodman. Yes. Thank you." The clerk hung up. "Number ten."

Outside in the twilight, a blond Adonis of a maintenance man was replacing a solar light next to the flagged path leading to the units. Beverly Hills teemed with beautiful creatures awaiting a call from the studios.

Number ten—identified by wrought-iron script above the door—was a one-story cottage with pale yellow siding. A security lamp sprang on when he mounted the low porch, and an instant later Teddie Goodman stood framed in the open doorway. She wore green silk lounging pajamas and tiny green slippers with gold butterflies on the toes. Silhouetted against artificial light, one hand resting on the doorframe, she struck him as even smaller than he'd thought; the impression she created of a tall woman was purely a matter of personality.

"If that filthy package contains a precious film, you know nothing about your job."

He glanced down at the tattered mailer under his arm as if he'd forgotten it was there.

"It doesn't. You can't have *Cleopatra*."

"You came all this way just to tell me that? You could have called and left a message."

"Wrong again. Movies come and go. Last year's Holy Grail is this year's $4.99 item in the bargain bin at Best Buy. I've come with what you really want." He patted the package.

She pursed her lips and stepped aside from the door.

It was all one room, divided only by a folding screen decorated with a watercolor Japanese landscape, delicate and very old. Whatever she had in the way of sleeping and toilet arrangements would lie on the other side. The rest was done entirely in white: A broad divan, tea tables, scattered fur rugs, stemmed lamps, a cabinet stereo playing something low from the era of crinolines and codpieces; all as pale and antiseptic as a snowdrift. Only a Yeti would find comfort there.

And he didn't buy it. No one, not even a Teddie Goodman, could keep up such an act consistently in every area of her life; it would be no life at all. The room was a prop, designed by an art director on a 1930s soundstage. There would be—there must be—an ordinary apartment hidden behind that screen

where she lived when she wasn't *on*, with a reclining chair, a
TV, and a meatloaf baking in the oven.

Above a porcelain fireplace hung a full-length oil portrait
of Theda Bara, dressed conservatively for her in an off-the-
shoulder claret-colored evening gown, one hand resting on an
enormous world globe—a movie prop, likely. The face bore an
unmistakable resemblance to Teddie's, but he had a sneaking
suspicion it had been retouched by an expert; a desperate attempt to bolster her claim to a blood relationship. He found this
latest evidence of her obsession encouraging.

She herself stood in the middle of the room, hip shot, one
arm across her middle gripping the opposite elbow, waiting.

Not knowing what else to do—in his haste he'd worked out
his approach only up to this moment—her visitor reached inside the mailer, drew out the brown shawl Henry Anklemire
had given him, and let it fall open, unfurling like a stage curtain
from his chest to his ankles. He set the empty package aside.

Had he not had so many run-ins with her in the past, Valentino might have missed it; an almost infinitesimal widening
of her eyes. For once in their acquaintance she'd let her professional mask slip.

"Where did you get that?"

She'd recognized the item, and it had caught her up short;
she hadn't time to dissemble.

He knew then he had her—if only he played things right. For
the first time in their long struggle, the game was his to lose.

He told her Anklemire's story.

"Convincing enough," she said, when he finished. She'd recovered her icy calm. "As far as anyone can rely on the word of
a man who lies for a living."

"Only for a living. He gave it to me with no strings attached."

"In that case, I'm sure a collector would be thrilled to own it."

The emphasis on *collector*—gentle as it was—placed that

creature somewhere among the lower animals. All the Holly-wood treasures that passed through her hands wound up the property of the corporation she worked for. Sentiment was a four-letter word in her dictionary.

He reversed the shawl, exposing the cinnamon-colored stain on that side.

"Blood," he said. "Human. I can show you the report from the UCLA lab if you like."

That bluff was the risky part. Arranging a chemical analysis and waiting for the results would have taken time he didn't have. He was banking a lot on Henry Anklemire's word, and Teddie's acceptance of his own.

He rushed on, before she could pose a question. "She told him she'd pricked herself once pinning it on."

She showed no reaction, but he nodded as if she had.

"You're way ahead of me, of course. A single lock of Beethoven's hair told scientists plenty about him after two hundred years. This stain's less than seventy. It ought to prove whether you're a relative of Theda Bara's or just another phony in a town top-heavy with them—if you're willing to trade.

"So what do you say, Teddie? Feeling lucky?"

33

TEDDIE COMMUNICATED AS much by silence as she did with words; she had that much in common at least with her namesake. The manner in which she relieved him of the shawl indicated neither acceptance nor rejection of his proposition. She carried it to one of the carved cabinets, a secretary with a writing surface beneath a two-door cupboard, which when she opened it revealed two shelves of thick volumes bound in uniform black. Embossed on the spines were figures he recognized as dates and production numbers, each book identified by the name of a studio, some of which had ceased to exist a century ago.

Where *did* she get her information? He'd wasted hundreds of hours trying to track down some of those figures on the Internet.

She traced the spines with an exquisitely manicured finger, slid out the one she wanted, spread it open on the desk, drew up a white slipper chair, and sat before it, the shawl folded on her lap. It was a loose-leaf notebook filled almost to bursting with glossy photographs encased in transparent plastic. Valentino was familiar with some of the publicity stills, but many were new to him: Originals, he noted, by way of numbers and titles hand-lettered on the borders by clerical workers long since dead, with the productions identified by title and stern warnings that the photos were the property of Fox Films and not to be removed from the studio. That volume alone had to have taken years to assemble.

A white-enameled Art Deco clock on the fireplace mantel ticked away five minutes while she paged through the leaves. At length she came to one marked *A Woman's Resurrection*. Unlike most, which featured the star of the movie in question posing among a group of fellow cast members, this one contained only the full figure of Theda Bara in one of her earliest performances, standing impossibly erect and staring out at the observer with eyes that still blazed across a gulf of more than ten decades. She was clutching a long wrap with a talon-like hand at her throat. Valentino was so caught up in the image he failed to take notice of the garment's singular weave until Teddie produced a magnifying lens, raised the shawl from her lap, and held it up to the photo, comparing the patterns through the glass.

Peering, she muttered, more to herself than to her visitor; she might have been alone in the room. "Never appeared in the film; or anywhere else, except here and in private."

Finally she appeared to remember his presence and raised her voice. "A gift from a sheikh of some sort, a harem brat ninety times removed from the throne. Fell in love with her image projected on a bedsheet in a tent theater in Marrakech or somesuch place and sent it to her along with a proposal of marriage; I think the gift itself is supposed to be a symbol of betrothal. My guess is it wound up on the cutting-room floor so Horny-el-Habib wouldn't take it as a yes."

She put down the lens and slammed shut the book. Smoothing the shawl across her lap, she looked at him with the same deep-set predatory eyes of the studio photo. *By God*, he thought, *if she isn't, she oughtta be.*

"I don't suppose there's a letter of provenance, or anything else to prove who it belonged to. Or are you holding back?"

"No to both. Does it matter?"

"Of course it does! You couldn't have lasted this long in the business without knowing that."

"As someone told me recently, we're not in court. When we spoke today I got the impression *you're* the only one who has to know. If a sample from your veins matches the genetic material on that shawl, no one on earth can prove you're wrong."

She sat stroking the stained corner of the garment between thumb and forefinger.

"This better be genuine," she said. "If it turns out one of Anklemire's disgruntled customers gave him a bloody nose, I'll ruin you."

"No dice, Teddie. I can't guarantee that either. It's Henry's word or nothing."

"*A Fool There Was*," she said after a moment. "A fool I am."

Letting go of the shawl, she manipulated something that popped open a compartment hidden in the scrollwork under the shelves, took out a key on a silken tassel, and unlocked a drawer next to her knee. From this she took a square sheet of heavy bond and turned his way, holding it out. When he reached to take it, she withdrew it, creased the sheet straight across on the edge of the desk, and tore off the top; the initials TG were engraved on it in entwined letters. This went into a white wicker wastebasket in the kneehole of the desk.

Still she held back the sheet. "No one's to know where this came from."

"Agreed."

She hesitated another half-second, then placed it in his hand.

"It was still current as of two days ago. I can't be responsible for where she is now."

He looked at it. The name and address were written in characters almost identical to those in her letterhead. He spoke the name for only the second time since he'd first seen it. It sounded strange coming from his mouth. "Carla Schmeisser."

AS USUAL, THE answer he'd sought so long only stoked his curiosity.

How had Teddie managed to cross paths with Leo Kalishnikov's daughter, when neither he nor Valentino suspected she was anywhere near California? But he knew from experience as well as instinct that Teddie had given up all she was going to give.

In any case he hadn't time to put that to the test. An old man was in jail, saddled with a crime he wasn't capable of committing, and every minute he spent in a cell with only his thoughts for company was as much a death sentence as any judge could hand down.

The photo ID displayed by the taxi driver who came for Valentino looked suspiciously like a headshot from an actor's résumé; the man himself resembled an advertisement for cosmetic surgery. When they stopped in front of the address in a residential section of Glendale, a two-story brick house on a shady street with a ROOMS FOR RENT sign in a window, Valentino told the driver to wait.

He was glad he did. The tall black woman who answered the door didn't know who Carla Schmeisser was, but after looking at her photo said, "That's Miss Simmons. She moved out yesterday."

"Did she leave a forwarding address?"

She shook her head.

"Did she go away in a taxi?"

"Yes."

"Do you remember the number?"

Another head shake.

"What company?"

This time she shrugged.

He was turning away, shoulders sagging, when she said, "All I know is a strange old man got out to help her with her things."

He turned back. "Strange how?"

"He was dressed like a pimp: You know, a white hat and a white suit."

He forced himself to speak slowly and carefully. "Did you happen to notice if he had a Russian accent?"

"He didn't say anything; but if he did, it wouldn't surprise me if it was in Klingon." She shook her head again. "Seriously, a nut job, all in white! Am I the only one around here who's not in show business?"

He was almost back in the cab before he remembered to shout out his thanks.

34

THE KOREAN RESTAURANT looked as doubtful as ever, down to the almost entirely Occidental clientele visible through the front window; rather than chance the bill of fare, local Asian-Americans took their appetites halfway across town. Valentino climbed the narrow staircase from the street and knocked on the door to Leo Kalishnikov's apartment. When no one responded after the second time, he tried the knob. It turned freely and the door pulled away from the frame. He leaned inside.

"Hello?"

Nothing had changed in the layout itself. It still resembled the set of *The Scarlet Empress*: some West Coast–bound art director's notion of a Russia that had never existed, at least not in the same place and all at one time. However, something was different from the archivist's last visit, and it took him a moment to identify just what.

The tenant's personal crisis had disturbed the order of the room along with his dress and grooming; the disheveled books and bric-a-brac on the shelves, the accumulation of dust, and the overlay of stale vodka, had made one think less of an imperial palace and more of a fraternity house on the morning after a toga party. Since then, someone had straightened up the place, setting right the knickknacks, vacuuming the upholstery and rugs, and dusting all the horizontal surfaces. Even the air had been freshened with some kind of citrus scent.

He stepped across the threshold, called out "Hello" again.

A beaded curtain across from the door crashed open and a woman charged out, holding a brass statuette of some mythical beast cocked over one shoulder, all horns and wings and claws, a lethal weapon on every surface. Her face was distended in a grimace of fear, rage, and savage intent.

Acting from blind reflex, Valentino threw up one hand and grasped the sculpture by the neck, halting its descent.

The woman countered with a sharp kick to his shin.

"Friend!" Tears in his eyes, he took hold of her other arm, restraining her even as he was hopping about on one foot. "Carla! I'm Valentino, Leo's friend! I'm not going to hurt you!"

She struggled another moment, then subsided, to his immense relief; she was small but strong.

Kalishnikov's glass-blue eyes stared at him. "You're Valentino?"

"Yes."

The rigidity went out of her arms. He released his grip and the statuette fell to her side. Any impression of slightness that might have been created by Carla Schmeisser's slender form was deceptive. Her bare arms were smoothly muscled, the green tank top she wore over a sports bra snug enough to reveal the taut concavity of her stomach. She'd appeared taller in her picture, but that was because she was built in even proportions. Her hair was strawberry blond, came just short of her shoulders, and she had her mother's chin, a straight nose that was all hers, and toned calves in black tights below the hem of her plain skirt. Her feet were small in custom-built running shoes: Air Jordans they were not.

He didn't need all that evidence to convince him she was athletic. His shin was still throbbing, little bolts of lightning spiking from the blade of the bone as in a comic strip.

"Who were you expecting?" he said.

"I—don't know. Leo—my father—told me not to open the door to anyone. He said there was something he had to do, and I'd hear from him soon. When I didn't, I had to go down to the sidewalk for air to keep from going crazy. After I came back I didn't realize I'd forgotten to lock the door until you"—she stopped, looked down—"is your leg all right? I'm so sorry."

Any resentment he might have felt evaporated when he heard her speak. Her frank Midwestern accent, so like his own, carried the essence of sincerity, and her rally to action in the presence of an intruder had impressed him. Harriet and Fanta, even the formidable Ruth, had nothing on this woman's native grit.

"Don't worry; I always carry a spare." Smiling, he gripped her shoulders again, gently this time. "You didn't do anything wrong. I shouldn't have barged in."

She saw she was still holding the bludgeon. Turning, she stood it on Kalishnikov's massive desk, where it was right at home among the gargoyles carved from the mahogany. She led him to the divan where the mock Muscovite had received him in uncharacteristically shabby dress, reeking of pure grain alcohol— was that only days ago? It was B.C.: before *Cleopatra*, before corpse, before Clifford, before calamity, chaos, and collaboration with the enemy. Time in crisis was relative.

She sat facing him in three-quarter profile, her knees pressed tight and her hands folded in her lap. "I don't know how much you know."

"I know your father's not Russian, about that fatal love triangle, and the trouble it got him into even though he was innocent. I know he was being blackmailed." He hesitated, then:

"Neither of us was sure but that you might have been behind it. That was before Jasper Grote entered the picture."

"That wasn't his name."

"I know that too. How did you know him?"

"He came to my place in Omaha, showed me that tin badge, and said that old homicide investigation had been reopened and the law would go easier on Leo—my father; I'm not used to calling him that—if he turned himself in. All I had to do was tell Grote where he could be found and Grote would escort him back home, where he'd have the chance to clear himself. I told him Leo left my mother before I was born and that I'd had no communication with him since. Grote changed his story then. He knew where my father was and that he was Leo Kalishnikov, the famous theater designer, but I could spare the taxpayers the expense of a trial if I paid Grote for his time and we'd forget all about it.

"I threw him out and called the police. They didn't tell me anything I hadn't already figured out on my own: His description didn't match anyone with the department."

"But you'd been in communication with Kalishnikov. You sent him back his check with the envelope unopened."

"He was a stranger. My mother never mentioned him beyond telling me his name when I asked who my father was; his *real* name. I didn't know about the other until that check came. Yes, I opened it; 'Kalishnikov' meant nothing to me and I was curious. When I read the note he sent with it, I sealed it back up and wrote RETURN TO SENDER on the envelope. As far as I knew, he'd abandoned my mother and me, and I wasn't about to let that man buy himself into my affections."

"What changed your mind?"

"I Googled him. He must appear at least a thousand times on the Web. Once I'd started to read about him I couldn't stop.

After a while I began to recognize the buffoonery—the absurd costumes, the burlesque accent—for what it was, just a gimmick to attract business. I saw a sensitive artist, a man with pride in his profession who nonetheless had a living to make. I understood then how important it was for him to disguise the fact that he cared about his work; to avoid being taken advantage of by the predatory types he came into contact with out here.

"I have Olympic aspirations," she said with a faint blush; "tennis. I've learned during interviews to put up a show of confidence to cover up my insecurities. He was doing the same thing, just in an overblown, California way.

"And I knew then he hadn't deserted us at all. We were too much alike for me to accept that picture as anything but a pose. He separated himself from us to spare Mother and me the pain and disgrace of being connected with a criminal in the eyes of the public."

A tight bitter smile came to her face. "Out here, a sinister reputation can be a plus. Back home it's just the opposite."

"We're not all quite as shallow as that," Valentino said. "But it's true a lot of us confuse scoundrelly behavior with worldliness."

She nodded absently; clearly what he'd said meant nothing to her. "Well, the police got back to me. They'd connected Jasper Grote with a petty crook named Harvey Handy, and wanted to know how I knew him and if I knew where he was. I said he was some braggart who'd flashed a badge in a bar, hoping to impress me—the real story was none of their business anymore—and that I had no idea where he'd gone.

"That was true at the time. Later it struck me that after I sent him packing, he thought he might as well go to Hollywood and try his luck there."

"That wasn't the only reason," Valentino said. "He sent a veiled blackmail demand to Kalishnikov over his computer, so you're right about that. But he left Nebraska as much to flee a charge of forgery as to dig for California gold; and when he got here, I was the first one he approached in person, using a film he happened to have, one he knew I'd want, probably to entice me into applying pressure to Leo. Apparently our Mr. Grote was the kind of snake that likes to come at you from the side."

She looked down at her hands, perhaps to still her fidgeting fingers. Then she looked up, her impossibly blue eyes as big as planets.

"I know about *Cleopatra*. Did it come yet?"

He goggled. For the second time in minutes he felt as if he'd been struck.

"It was you who sent it? But, how—?"

Her expression, unusual for her, was illegible. Then, without changing, it was as clear to him as a highway marker.

This was life, not a movie. Seated before a motion-picture screen, a flash of understanding sent a thrill to one's imagination. Here in Leo Kalishnikov's apartment—as exotic as it was, he was obliged to pay rent on it the first of every month just like everyone else—Valentino felt a surge of nausea.

"You were there," he said. "You saw Grote die."

Her eyes remained on his, steady: Twin spheres frozen in mid-orbit. "I killed him."

35

WHEN IT CAME to drinking, Valentino had no Olympic aspirations; but at that moment his gaze wandered toward the fat, short-necked bottle on a shelf of foreign texts with a Russian bear on the label.

Which was as far as he got. Half a glass of anything had been known to pack him off to bed, and if ever a conversation required sober focus, this was it. He clasped both her hands in his. Sergeant Clifford had used the same gesture to break down his defenses; he did it to strengthen Carla's.

"Tell me as much as you want. You have no reason to trust me, I know; but we're the only ones here. If I were to tell anyone, it'd be your word against mine, and I'm already in the doghouse so far as the law is concerned."

"I *can* trust you," she said. "At least I think so. You turned up in so much of the material I found on my father. A man as obviously sincere as you were in interviews about your hopes for your theater is a man I'll take a chance on. Also you have an honest face. Golly, I'm pure Nebraska, aren't I?" Consciously or not, her accent took on a twang. Then it was gone.

"When I realized Grote would be coming here to try the same thing on my father he tried on me, I came out myself. I didn't tell anyone I was coming, not even Leo. How could I expect him to believe I wasn't in on the blackmail scheme, so many years after I rejected him without a word? I had no right to assume he'd be any more welcoming to me than I'd been to him. So I, um, rented a room I could afford for a base of operations."

That *um* caught his attention, but he didn't want to interrupt her in mid-flow. He inserted a bookmark for later reference.

She said, "He's listed here, under his business. For two days I watched the place, thinking I might spot Grote going in or coming out, but then I got restless. I went from there to your office building at the university, but the only person I recognized using the entrance was you, from your pictures. Next I tried your theater—" She frowned. "The Orifice?"

He winced. "Oracle."

"It was closed for renovations. That dead end almost sent me packing; but I remembered an article I read about you that mentioned you had a woman friend, a medical examiner with the police department. I couldn't remember her name, but I found it on my computer back in the apartment."

"How'd you get Harriet's address? Police personnel are unlisted, for obvious reasons."

She blushed a second time; on her, it was attractive.

"Well, I haven't seen nearly as many movies as you, but I guess I've learned enough from them to pull off a bluff. I got through to Forensics, said I'm her sister who's visiting from out of town and I lost her address. I guess being frustrated for days made my tears sound real, so the clerk or whatever gave me the number of her building, but not her condo. I guess he was leaving that up to whoever I spoke to there; you know, passing the buck in case it came back on him."

Valentino smiled tentatively; making a note to have a firm

conversation with Harriet's manager. "But being by now an experienced stakeout artist," he said, "the building was all you needed."

She nodded. "I wasn't in place half an hour when I saw him go in. Just in case I was mistaken, I stayed put until he came out, which was in less than fifteen minutes. It was him, all right; you don't see characters like that anyplace but where I came from, and not so many there, anymore. He'd be right at home in a documentary about the Dust Bowl."

Valentino made a fast inventory of the information at hand. "That would have been, let's see: Monday morning?"

"Yes! Is that when you met him?"

"No. He left a message at the office and when I didn't answer he went to Harriet's. Someone must have told him I was staying there temporarily, maybe one of the workers at the Oracle. He missed me. I take it you followed him from the condo building."

"I did. I'm driving just about the most invisible car Enterprise has in stock. He was staying at a motel called the Nomad, with a sign out front advertising cable in every room, like it was just invented. I thought about moving there, but all the rooms look out on the parking lot and the chances of him spotting me were too great, so I went back to Glendale every night and set up shop across from the Nomad every morning. I wanted to see if he made contact with you or my father before I went to the police. I knew they wouldn't question either of you without proof he'd approached you."

"Proof like a picture?"

She slid a sleek phone from a pocket of her skirt and held it up.

He had a sudden inspiration. "May I see that?"

"It won't tell you anything. I never was able to get a shot of him with you or Leo."

"May I?" he said again, raising a hand.

Frowning again, she laid it in his palm. He swiped the screen, pausing just long enough to identify tourist-type snaps of palm trees on Sunset, bathers off Malibu, Paramount's iconic main gate, the heart-stopping spectrum of the sun extinguishing itself in the Pacific, stopping at last on a pastoral pose: an attractive, well-toned young lady in a silver jogging suit leaning against a tree on a grassy slope he now knew belonged to Griffith Park. He showed it to her. "Who took this? No, never mind. Tell me later. So you were still following Grote around when he went to East L.A."

"Y-yes." Her chin quivered. "He was carrying a package when he got off the bus, all taped up in some kind of plastic mesh. I guessed what it was, and I knew he was there to make a trade: *Cleopatra* in return for his payoff. Whatever the film's worth, he stood to squeeze a lot more from my father over his lifetime. It was clear then who he was there to meet; Leo didn't share your interest in film, only the places where they were shown.

"I was careless," she said. "When he started toward that underground theater, I got out to follow him on foot. The dome light came on; he must've seen it out of the corner of his eye. He turned, spotted me, and reached under his coat. When he saw who it was, he must've thought I was there to stop him any way I could, so I—I guess he was acting in self-defense. I panicked when I saw the gun. I—" She stopped. Her throat worked. She straightened her shoulders; steeling herself, an athlete preparing for the contest. Her tone steadied. "I couldn't jump back into the car; I'd make too good a target under the dome. There was no place in that open area to run. No place except straight ahead. It was like charging the net. I hit him as hard as I'd ever swung at the ball, with my whole body, driving it like—like a bullet." She nodded, a definite gesture. "Like a bullet. I didn't even hear the shot."

NO PLACE IN that city was ever completely still. The threshing of traffic on the freeways, the hiccup of an air conditioner coming to life, the thud of a bass beat from a passing van, the ambient air stirring in a room, were constants; but they took on significance only when conversation stopped, and then they were as profound as silence. When Valentino broke it, it was as much to relieve the pressure as to obtain information.

"Why did you put him in my car?"

"I didn't know it was yours. I'd never seen it. I panicked. If I were found with the—the body, I'd be arrested and identified, and then the whole thing would come out; my father would be ruined. Even if his innocence were proved, the fact that he'd changed his name and his manner and lied about his past would make him guilty in most people's eyes—not a self-promoting businessman, but a fugitive with something shameful to hide. I couldn't be the one who brought that on him. The car was close and it was unlocked. After that was done I saw Grote's gun on the ground where he'd—where *we'd* dropped it. I scooped it up and threw it as far as I could into the shadows."

"It was far enough the police didn't find it for days," he said. "You've got one heck of a serve."

36

HE FOUND HIMSELF watching her; it was like taking a closer look at an Old Master to determine if it was genuine. Was this the face of a killer?

"You took away the film," he said. "What did you have in mind?"

"Nothing. I didn't realize I had it until I reached for him—his body—and there it was in my arms. He must have let go of it in the scuffle and I caught it without thinking. I put it aside, but I picked it up later and took it back to my car. I wasn't sure but that there might be something in the package that would incriminate my father. When I opened the package back in the apartment and saw what it was, there seemed only one thing to do with it, so I sent it to you at the university."

He remembered then he was still holding her phone. He returned it. "Who took that picture of you?"

"Oh—that. A stranger. I was taking a walk and I found a spot I liked. She was kind enough to do me the favor."

She.

"Where was it?"

"I forget. It wasn't long after I got here, and I wandered around a lot, getting my bearings. It was just a pleasant place, away from all the cloverleafs and high-rises. It reminded me of home. I guess I was homesick."

"It's Griffith Park. The observatory's just visible in one corner. It's not far from the room you rented in the house in Glendale. Nice neighborhood."

"It is. I was lucky to find it."

"Nobody recommended it?"

"No. I just saw the sign when I was driving around."

"Kind of pricey. Not on the scale of Beverly Hills, but a long way from a dump like the Nomad Motel. What do you do for a living, Carla? Not tennis. You have to maintain your amateur status if you're going to compete in the Olympics."

"I work at a medical clinic in Omaha. I'm a receptionist. I had a lot of vacation time built up, but it runs out next week. I—guess I don't have to worry about that now, do I?" She managed a pathetic smile.

"Counting the flight here, the cost of renting a car, and the price of things in our fair city in general, an address in Glendale is a luxury. You hesitated before when you said you'd rented a room. Who's picking it up?"

She surprised him, meeting his gaze head on.

"Why ask a question you know the answer to already? Miss Goodman told you where I was staying or you wouldn't have traced me here."

Valentino regrouped. He'd only expected to hit a nerve; but if it was a fight she wanted, so be it.

"Next you'll tell me that kind stranger you got to take your picture just happened to be Teddie Goodman. She wandered along purely at random while you were taking in the sights; the one person in Los Angeles who completes the circuit between Leo Kalishnikov, *Cleopatra*, Jasper Grote, and me."

"No, I'm not going to tell you that. In fact I'm not going to tell you anything more. I opened up to you, thinking you wanted to help me and my father, but you're acting like a policeman. I thought you were his friend."

"I am. I'm here because he asked for my help; he'd have told you that. Where do you think he went after he brought you here, where the police wouldn't be looking for you, because their chief suspect was already in custody?"

She paled. "What do you mean, in custody?"

"Your father told the police he killed Grote. That check you sent back? He's waited all these years to make good on it."

Her face collapsed. Valentino was ready for that. He got up, poured two inches apiece of Russian Bear into a pair of glasses he found in the kitchen, and handed her one. The raw vodka scraped his throat like ground glass. Hers, too, from the way her color came back.

It came out then.

BACKED BY THE Supernova treasury, Teddie Goodman's records would have been the envy of J. Edgar Hoover. She was a scavenger by trade, gathering morsels of interest involving everyone and everything connected with the motion-picture industry, from studio brass to the busboys in the commissary and all the satellites that circulated in its orbit. This was speculation based on facts Carla couldn't have known, filling in gaps in her narrative.

Teddie knew of Kalishnikov's past in Nebraska. The scandal was public knowledge there, and needed only a researcher with her determination to establish the link to his life in California; the dates of a murder suspect's flight from prosecution back east and of the putative Russian's sudden appearance in L.A. society coincided too neatly to ignore. Once the connection was confirmed, it joined her files until such time as it might prove useful.

She had, by her own admission, tried to acquire *Cleopatra*, probably after having received a query from Grote, only to walk away because the price was unreasonable; likely she suspected a scam. But she overlooked nothing. After returning home she monitored his movements, and when they led him to the Coast, she combed through her files. There was Nebraska, and there Kalishnikov.

"How'd she find you?" Valentino asked Carla.

"She wouldn't say. All I know is she approached me while I was leaving the Visitors Council my first day in town and gave me her card. She said all she was interested in was *Cleopatra*, that she'd missed her chance the first time and that if I agreed to put her back on the scent she'd put me up at a comfortable place while I made my search for Grote. We went to Griffith Park—yes, I lied to you about not knowing where it was—and took my picture in case she wanted to approach my father and needed proof she'd found me. A neutral place, she called it, so he wouldn't know where to look for me based on the location."

Neutral place, he thought; Teddie's exact words, back at The Oracle. No wonder she hadn't been surprised when he'd suggested it.

"I couldn't refuse," Carla said. "I'd just found out how expensive it is to stay here even temporarily. She said she couldn't help me search because she was too busy to spend time on such an iffy enterprise, but it was worth the cash outlay on the off chance I came through. When I asked how she knew so much about me, she just smiled and put her finger to her lips. I know it sounds like I'm making all this up—"

He interrupted. "Actually, you just convinced me. Given the choice between open and mysterious, Teddie will take mysterious every time, even if the other way is easier. Nobody who hadn't actually bargained with her would invent such a story. But if you had an arrangement, why did you send *Cleopatra* to me instead of her?"

"It was what you said, that mysterious quality of hers. I saw nothing in her face to compare with what I'd seen in yours, in all those pictures. I suppose I was still in shock, but after it passed, after the thing was done, I still felt the same way. Um, I suppose now I'll have to repay her for my bill."

"That's up to you, but I wouldn't feel obligated. She took that picture of you—on her cell, not yours—to use as bait to reel me in, just in case you slipped the hook. They don't call it double-dealing for nothing."

That weak smile fluttered back. She'd set down her glass in the same spot on the rug where her father had stood his bottle; he retrieved it and pressed it into her hands. She drank off the rest in one long draught and put it back, this time with no sign of its earlier effect.

"You don't believe me, and I don't blame you. Now that I've said it all aloud, it makes even less sense."

He shook his head. "If it didn't, I might not. The truth never hangs together quite as much as a well-crafted lie. And if I know Sergeant Clifford, she'll accept it.

"It has to come from you," he said, when she stiffened. "I'd say that even if I hadn't promised to keep quiet myself, and I will. She'll see that Leo lied to protect you, and she'll know you told the truth to protect *him*. *Two* lies would just cancel each other out, and she'd be left with an unsolved case." He looked down at his glass, but the contents appeared more toxic than ever. He set it down beside hers.

"You called your father." It was a guess, but in expressing it he knew it for a certainty.

"Yes. He didn't even let me explain over the phone. He came to get me right away. He *is* a good man, isn't he? I wasn't wrong."

"You weren't wrong. You may hold the record for making poor choices—although I think you and I are in a tie there—but who else could you go to if not your only flesh and blood? My honest face in a photograph can only take you so far."

He stood, holding out his hand. "Get your things while I call a cab. I'm temporarily without wheels, and I suppose your rental's back in Glendale. As they say in the movies, we're going downtown."

"Would my things include a toothbrush?"

He laughed, it was so absurd. "I don't think so. When Clifford hears your story, she'll probably offer you a lift back home."

"Back here, you mean. This is home."

"I thought that was clear." But he was glad she'd said it.

He helped her up. He felt a rush of optimism: Maybe the gift of Theda Bara's genes would wipe out Teddie's resentment over the loss of a few hundred feet of ancient celluloid. It seemed to be a case for family reconciliations.

37

NEON SCRAPED A shocking blue-green arch against a purple sky, igniting the orb at the end in an explosion of pink script: THE COMET. Stars showered down like fireworks and the cycle began all over again.

The woman in the ticket booth, wearing a metallic jump suit and a bubble helmet, glanced at the pass Fanta handed her through the driver's side window, directed her to the slot reserved for her car, and raised the barricade. The car crept down the center aisle and turned where indicated. It sat idling while a teenage boy in similar costume hastened to remove a pair of orange cones. He guided the vehicle into the space.

"I never thought I'd say this," Fanta said: "Welcome, Pacific Standard Time."

"Strange talk, from a fully indoctrinated sun-worshipper." Kyle Broadhead, seated in the passenger's seat next to his wife, tugged his tweed hat down over his ears and fastened the top button of his old black overcoat. The dashboard thermometer read sixty-two, and although that was chilly by local standards even in October, the professor's face was as red as a fireplug.

He insisted he'd left his core temperature behind in a Cold War dungeon.

Fanta laced her arm inside his. "We'll get you a nice hot cup of cocoa as soon as the late arrivals kill their engines. Meanwhile—" She leaned over from behind the wheel and switched on the blower. The air in the car, a fleet vehicle belonging to the law firm where she worked, warmed and filled with the scorched-metal smell of a heater disused since January.

Harriet, huddled close to Valentino in the back seat, said, "Kyle, you know as well as I do your child bride comes by her color through heredity. She's too busy gathering evidence against video hackers to waste time on the beach. She was referring to the early dusk. Daylight Savings Time is poison to a drive-in theater. Kids have to be in bed before midnight."

"I owe Dinky lunch at Chasen's," Valentino said, looking out at the rows of vehicles parked facing The Comet's mammoth inflatable screen, others pulling in beside them. "I never thought he'd open before the end of the year."

"You're lucky I didn't make it La Scala."

The contractor had come to the archivist's window, which remained open; like most of the party, he lacked Broadhead's colorful (and possibly exaggerated) past. Schwartz looked more out of place than ever in full evening dress, his muscular neck red as a boiled lobster against his stiff white collar.

Broadhead pointed at him with the stem of his pipe—cold for once, by popular demand. "Wherever did you find a soup-and-fish so far outside Oscar season? You look like a truck driver at his daughter's wedding."

"And yet I don't feel inconspicuous." Schwartz inclined his head toward the vehicle parked in the slot next to theirs: a black-and-chromium Rolls-Royce Silver Ghost with a hood as long as a locomotive boiler, a liveried chauffeur in a seat open to the elements, and Leo Kalishnikov in the coach behind, pouring champagne into a flute with Carla Schmeisser seated at his side. Her simple evening frock faded into the background next to her father's tall Astrakhan hat and scarlet tunic trimmed with gold frogs.

"Henry Anklemire could take lessons in Chutzpah from that old Cossack," said Broadhead. "Probably has his horse stashed in the trunk."

Valentino and Harriet shared a smile. In dismissing all charges against Carla in the Grote killing, Sergeant Clifford had kept Kalishnikov's involvement from the press, his past included. ("They know about Grote," she'd said. "Who cares about a dead con man? One more unsolved murder won't make a dent in my arrest record.") The Russian charade went on without interruption. For once, however, the flamboyant theater designer looked ill at ease beneath the bluster, as did his companion. Father and daughter were still getting to know each other.

Harriet patted her date's arm; she'd read his mind. "They'll get there. You can't go from Omaha to Hollywood overnight."

"But you can go from Hollywood to Cincinnati in less time than that. Did you see *E.T.* last night?"

She laughed. "I didn't know where to look: Teddie Goodman in one of her *haute couture* nightmares, or the mayor of Cincinnati handing her the key to the city wearing a metal bra with a snake to match on his head. He must not be running for re-election."

"Actually, he's ahead in the polls. The Midwest is changing: Grote types are almost extinct. Anyway, film preservation made out like a bandit. UCLA has another jewel in its crown, *plus* a parade in Theda Bara's hometown pumping up publicity for *Cleopatra*'s art-house tour across the U.S. And I won't stop looking for those other reels. Not a bad return for a second-hand shawl."

Although the mainstream media had at first ignored the

results of Teddie's independent DNA test, Twitter, YouTube, and a swarm of podcasts had pronounced her the reincarnation of the greatest vamp of all time. She'd made Page Two of *Parade*.

Dinky said, "I'm sorry I missed the grand re-opening."

"Me, too," Valentino said; "but I know you and Leo were busy with your own. The Oracle cleared enough the first night to cover the cost of the new bathroom. Kyle's buying our refreshments tonight, by the way; he bet me that the world premiere of a hundred-year-old film wouldn't fill half the seats in the house."

Broadhead blew his nose. "What's popcorn and soda for four compared to the artichoke dip at Chasen's?"

"The audience didn't riot when it found out the picture had no ending?" Dinky looked sober.

"I hired the university players to perform the last act from *Antony and Cleopatra*," Valentino said; "the first live show on that stage since nineteen-twenty-eight. It made such a hit Criterion's going to film it and put it on the DVD."

The contractor beamed; then he nodded over to the Rolls-Royce. "I must pay my respects to my partner. You folks enjoy the show."

After he left, Harriet leaned over the back of Fanta's seat. "So what was the paper gift on page eighty-seven of Kyle's manuscript?"

Broadhead answered. "A house; or rather the deed to a bungalow in Burbank. She's been after me to sell the place I shared with my first wife. I got a deal on this one. It's supposed to be haunted by a dress extra who hanged himself in the shower in nineteen-thirty-three, the day FDR was inaugurated. He was probably a Republican."

Valentino asked Fanta if she was going to re-do the bathroom.

"I haven't decided yet; maybe just a new shower curtain. I don't want to scare off my ghost. I've always wanted one."

Valentino saw a man in the aisle, spearing a crushed soda cup with a stick and depositing it in a black plastic trash bag; an unusual sight just before the first feature, and he wasn't in an employee uniform. Old and bent, he wore a brown sweater nearly as old as he was, heavy for the weather and hanging nearly to the crotch of his black sweatpants. Turning, he saw the archivist, smiled, and gave him a thumbs-up; he'd been recognized.

Valentino had almost forgotten the incident a week later, as he was packing to go back home to The Oracle. Harriet's TV was on with the sound turned off, but he spotted a familiar face in a recent photograph. He put down a stack of folded shirts, picked up the remote, and took the TV off mute in time to hear the female newscaster:

". . . Tobias Winters, the founder of L.A.'s first drive-in movie theater; one of California's last pioneers, dead of natural causes at ninety-nine."

Back at The Comet, Fanta switched on the car radio and tuned it to the theater frequency. Tinny music came up to accompany the animated snacks romping on the screen. Harriet snuggled closer to Valentino. "You're sure tonight's feature was the right choice to christen a place like the Comet? Young families are the target audience. Most of them have never seen a black-and-white movie, let alone . . ." She shrugged.

"Dink was adamant; and I feel sorry for saddling him with Kalishnikov, who can nit-pick you to death during construction. So I loaned him a crisp new print on safety stock. It ought to look stupendous on a screen the size of a football field."

"But it's so *old!*"

He squeezed her arm, silencing her. The drumbeat announcing an American International picture thundered from all the speakers. The title sprang on, a hundred yards wide and as tall as a two-story building:

I WAS A TEENAGE WEREWOLF

"After all," Valentino whispered, "it *is* that time of year."

CLOSING CREDITS

This section is unfortunately brief. Many of the sources consulted for *Vamp* have received mention in earlier books in the Valentino series, and reliable information on the movies of Theda Bara is spotty. Too many self-styled historians have never seen a single frame of her work, basing their opinions on the reports of predecessors (often lifting whole paragraphs from their reviews) and publicity stills, which provide a distorted picture of her career: In none of her surviving films, for instance, is she seen crouching among human skeletons.

The scarcity of footage (from an oeuvre of no less than forty movies!) is even more disappointing to the researcher. *Cleopatra,* Bara's signature film, is among the lost, and even *Hollywood,* Kevin Brownlow and David Gill's monumental multipart documentary on the silent cinema, contains neither a clip nor a mention of her name. Like the bewitching beauties she portrayed again and again, she remains a mystery—and an ideal quarry for Valentino.

BIBLIOGRAPHY

Amberg, George, editor. *The New York Times Reviews 1913–1970.* New York: Quadrangle, 1970.

Although this contains a review of only one Theda Bara film (*The Serpent*, 1916), the unsigned piece stands as a model of fairness and sly humor—even if a mouse seems to have stolen the picture!

Anderson, Mary Ann. "Nostalgic Drive-Ins Are Way to Find Romance on Four Wheels." Chicago: Tribune News Service, March, 2022.

A fine capsule description of this uniquely American phenomenon, with information on latter-day upgrades and advice on what to take and not to take to a showing.

Cameron, James R. *Motion Picture Projection and Sound Pictures.* Woodmont, Ct.: Cameron Publishing Co., 1944.

Updated and reissued nine times starting in 1918 (in sturdily bound editions with handsome jackets), Cameron's is one of the most reliable texts available to both projectionists and scholars, with step-by-step guides (accompanied by exploded-view illustrations of the necessary equipment) and a brief history of the technology. The chapter titled "Auto Drive-In Theaters" was invaluable in understanding the logistics of showing movies out-of-doors.

Drew, William M. *Speaking of Silents.* **Vestal, New York: Vestal Press, 1989.**
The mention is brief—only five lines of print—but Colleen Moore's fond memories of her friendship with Theda Bara are heartwarming, and evidence (contrary to the conclusions formed by gossipy "scholars") that she never fell for her own publicity.

Haggard, H. Rider. *Cleopatra.* **London: Longmans, Green & Co., 1899.**
Haggard's novel provided most of the storyline for the 1917 film adaptation. This dense but fascinating romance helps bridge the gap left by the film's unavailability. (In 1920, Haggard sued Fox for its "shameless plagiarism" of his book and collected 5,000 pounds.)

Higgins, D.S. *Rider Haggard: A Biography.* **New York: Stein and Day, 1981.**
Higgins' sensitive analysis of Haggard's working method details the exhaustive on-site research that went into *Cleopatra.*

Kotowski, Mariusz. *Pola Negri: Hollywood's First Femme Fatale.* **Lexington, Ky.: University Press of Kentucky, 2014.**
Although I take issue with his subtitle—Theda Bara invented the type years before Negri stepped onto a motion-picture set—Kotowski's book is a sympathetic and meticulously researched biography of a woman who shared Bara's experience in the limelight. His subject, frequently dismissed as a diva obsessed with her career, emerges here as a serious professional with a rich private life and, yes: a deep and lasting love for Rudolph Valentino, to whom she was engaged at the time of his death at age thirty-one. Her body of work, from *The Cheat* (1923) through

The Moon-Spinners (1964), tells us much about the fickle nature of fame that her contemporary knew so well.

Krefft, Vanda. *The Man Who Made the Movies: The Meteoric Rise and Tragic Fall of William Fox.* **New York: HarperCollins, 2017.**
This is a brilliant book, charting the steep parabola of Fox's pioneering career. (He's the inspiration for Max Fink, the flawed visionary behind The Oracle.) Krefft's grasp of the labyrinthine legal and corporate details of the studio's management, and her ability to explain them in layman's terms (without condescension), are essential to the study of the motion-picture industry during its formative years. Although Krefft buys into the narcissistic myth (based entirely on comments by Fox, who was held *all* actors in contempt), the book is a rich source of detail on the professional and private life of Theodosia Burr Goodman a/k/a Theda Bara. (And yes, the shawl is here!)

Newton, Michael, and Roger Savin, Project Consultants. *The Movie Book.* **London: Phaedra Press, Ltd., 1999.**
It's a coffee-table page-turner, lavishly illustrated and invaluable for quick-reference, CliffsNotes-type information on eleven decades of cinema history.

Pajer, Nichole. *Drive-Ins: An American Treasure. Parade,* **July 19, 2020.**
A feel-good puff piece, and more likely the product of wishful thinking than a report of an actual renaissance; but it's handy history, and—who knows?—may prove to be a self-fulfilling prophecy. Certainly the preponderance of these human-interest features suggests there is a groundswell of interest in vehicular viewing.

FILMOGRAPHY

Cleopatra. J. Gordon Edwards, director, written by Adrian Johnson, starring Theda Bara. Fox, 1917.

With a cast of twenty-five to thirty thousand, and stupendous sets representing Cleopatra's palace at Alexandria, eighty Roman galleons, and the Roman forum, built from 250,000 feet of lumber, it's a tragedy that no one has been able to see the feature since 1937, when a warehouse fire destroyed Fox's own print. Apart from a few seconds of footage discovered in 1974, nothing else appears to remain. The American Film Institute lists it among its nine "Most Wanted Lost Films." Lacking Valentino's access to the original, I had to re-create the experience from its literary sources: Haggard's *Cleopatra*, Shakespeare's *Antony and Cleopatra*, and Arthur Weigall's history *The Life and Times of Cleopatra*, as well as personal memoirs, period reviews, and publicity stills. Let's hope we don't have to wait another eighty-five years to appreciate the film firsthand.

Cleopatra. Directed by Cecil B. DeMille, written by Waldemar Young and Vincent Lawrence, starring Claudette Colbert, Warren William, Henry

Wilcoxon, Gertrude Michael, Joseph Schildkraut, C. Aubrey Smith, Clau-
dia Dell, and Robert Warwick. Paramount, 1934.

An intelligent and highly entertaining take on the (literally)
age-old story. It was released the same year as *It Happened One
Night*; viewers who know Colbert mostly as a comedic actress in
that Oscar winner may be surprised by her shrewd and haughty
Queen of the Nile. And thanks to DeMille—who almost certainly saw the 1917 version and took notes—we may glean some
notion of the character of the original production. (Endearingly,
DeMille cast the unknown Wilcoxon as Marc Antony because
he thought he had a head made to wear a helmet!) Available on
DVD.

Cleopatra. Joseph L. Mankiewicz, director, written by Joseph L. Mankie-
wicz, Ranald MacDougall, and Sidney Buchman, starring Elizabeth Tay-
lor, Richard Burton, Rex Harrison, Pamela Brown, George Cole, Hume
Cronyn, Cesare Danova, Kenneth Haigh, Andrew Keir, Martin Landau,
Carroll O'Connor, and Roddy McDowall. Twentieth-Century Fox, 1963.
Available on DVD.

Only Harrison and McDowall emerge from this four-hour
ordeal with any credit; although Taylor's contract, guaranteeing
bonuses for production delays (most of which sprang from her
own ailments), made her the first performer to earn more than
a million dollars for one picture. It flopped spectacularly, nearly
bankrupting Fox; but screening it may offer a clue as to why so
many critics panned the original—which nevertheless made a
smash hit at the box office. Available on DVD.

A Fool There Was. Frank Powell, director, starring Theda Bara and Frank
José, based on the play by Porter Emerson Browne. Fox, 1915.

Fortunately (miraculously!), Bara's first starring role has come
down to us intact. It has all the faults associated with films of
its era, also all the strengths attributed to it by Valentino (the

sublime "Kiss Me, My Fool!" has become part of our language); and it was Fox's first hit. The movies are the only art form we can see developing in real time; this is a prime example. It's like watching an Old Master painting his first canvas in stop-motion. Available on DVD.

Going Attractions: The Definitive Story of the American Drive-In Movie. April Wright, director. April Nine Entertainment, in Association with Dice Films, 2013.

Part hope—yards and yards of material on entrepreneurial efforts at a drive-in revival, with asides on improved technology—part tragedy—bleak images of Walmarts and parking structures standing on the sites of expired theaters—this lively documentary is a valuable contribution to popular-culture history, and to the concept of The Comet. Available on DVD.

I Was a Teenage Werewolf. Gene Fowler, Jr., director, written by Ralph Thornton, starring Michael Landon, Yvonne Lime, Whit Bissell, Vladimir Sokoloff, and Guy Williams. American International, 1957.

It's as emblematic as any of the kind of fare that played in most drive-ins during their heyday; and it's a guilty pleasure, especially at Halloween. Landon, of course, would go on to star in TV's *Bonanza, Little House on the Prairie,* and *Highway to Heaven*; and Williams in Walt Disney's *Zorro*. Whit Bissell may seem a bland choice for the mad scientist, but this veteran, likeable character actor has gone too long unsung.

Rebel Without a Cause. Nicholas Ray, director, written by Stewart Stern, starring James Dean, Natalie Wood, Sal Mineo, Jim Backus, Ann Doran, William Hopper, Rochelle Hudson, Corey Allen, Edward Platt, Dennis Hopper, Nick Adams. Warner Brothers, 1955.

It made icons of both Dean and the Griffith Observatory, scene of a teenage rumble and that dramatization of an exploding

earth that helped to explain the nihilistic attitude of the youthful cast. I seem to be in the minority, but I find Dean's acting
mannered and, when a display of emotion can't be avoided, his-
trionic. Mineo and Wood—two of the four players in this film
(including Dean) who died tragically before they could claim
Social Security—are standouts.

The Serpent. (Writer and director unknown.) Starring Theda Bara.

This one's gone; a shame, because it would be a treat to
watch the star winding men around her taloned little finger
against the backdrop of Imperial Russia, and transforming herself at the end, in a haze of smoke and artistic lighting, into the
Devil! (See *The New York Times Reviews* in the Bibliography.)